BLACKPOOL GIRL

by

Margaret Swainson

*A story of love,
that takes you to
exciting places.*

CONTENTS

CHAPTER 1

Home is where the heart is

My name is Leah Harris. My story is one of love, loss, laughter and life's adventures. Things are about to change. It may be for the better, it may be for the worst but change it must and I'm ready for everything that life may throw at me.

Following a long term unsuccessful relationship I resigned from the job that I loved, packed my bags, put on a brave face and now I'm venturing from my home town to London to make a new start.

Fortunately I have the strength and family support to do this. You are only on this earth once and so you need to make the most of it I told myself. Make the right friends, make the right choices and with a bit of luck you will lead a fulfilling life doing with it what you want. It's possible.

I was twenty seven and in good shape. I didn't smoke, drink too much, well not too often, or stay out all night. My figure was reasonably OK though a few pounds shed here and there wouldn't go amiss. I was always told that I had a nice smile and was a bubbly personality. So why had I been wasting my time on a failed romance? I asked myself. I think the answer was simply that I had been too busy as a nurse to notice. I was worth more than a second rate love, more than somebody who was merely an OK guy. I wanted love. Strong, deep love and I knew I had to get away for a complete new start to find it.

I packed my bags. "Don't forget to take your passport " reminded Mum. " You never know when you might need it." I looked at her hopefully......

I know that I shall miss my hometown of Blackpool. I was born and bred in this lively and exciting Lancashire town situated on the west coast of the UK. I'm proud of the area with the beautiful English countryside on our doorstep. We have both the sea and the countryside at our beckoning, so lucky.

The town of Blackpool is a larger than life place. It's known as the Las Vegas of the North. You need to see it for yourself.

There are plenty of places here to have that 'good time' like the Blackpool Tower and ballroom, famous from the TV's Strictly Come Dancing programme which is avidly watched by millions. Our Pleasure Beach, which is an amusement park, is one of the most visited tourist attractions in England. It's worth taking a look at its thrills and spills on the Internet. There are rides to suit all ages and levels of daringness; like the old flying machines from the early days or The Icon that will twist and turn you at high speeds until you are screaming and wishing it would stop.

On a sunny day beautiful soft golden sandy beaches lay between three amusement piers and invite you to lay down your towel and catch the warmth of the sun. Arcades are everywhere. You can lose your small change playing to win a few pence on the variety of brightly lit tempting games. Seaside donkeys, looking well fed and groomed offer beach rides to little ones. The donkeys are an old seaside treat, one that Blackpool is famed for. Blackpool rock and gaudy souvenirs are everywhere. Squawking seagulls hungry for titbits from the visitors fly high above. Take care or your ice cream will be swiftly taken from you when a bold seagull deftly swoops down for his tea.

Blackpool people come from many walks of life. The locals are warm, friendly salt of the earth types. No pretence there. The swarming visitors, like ants going in every direction, are all out to have as much fun as they can fit in. As you might expect a little tipple enhances their enjoyment. Then there are the hard workers, the strugglers, the family people, those who have to count the pennies and some who are lucky enough to have plenty.

There are quite a proportion of people in Blackpool who have had traumas in their lives and have problems that need addressing, poor souls. They look so downtrodden, often dirty, thin and malnourished, holding a can of strong lager, their most valuable possession.

The great majority of locals are helpful, friendly and have a great sense of humour, whether rich or poor. On a simple bus ride you can see conversations between strangers springing up with chuckling and laughter thrown into the mix. Visitors return time and time again to taste the hospitality and friendliness, drawn like a magnet.

So it is with a heavy and broken heart that I catch a ride on the famous seafront tram passing Blackpool sights. Farewell to the iconic Blackpool Tower rising to the sky, goodbye to the princess carriages decorated with fabric flowers thrilling lucky little children, au revoir to the noisy visitors with their children and pushchairs and cheers to the fortune teller touting for trade ...... I love it all.

I headed for Blackpool North station to leave my beloved Blackpool for a new life. My heart is thumping nineteen to the dozen and I feel a bit emotional. With grim determination and a tear trickling down my cheek I take this big step into an unknown future.

CHAPTER 2

Breaking up

I reached the station and dragging my heavy suitcase trundled towards the train. My train ticket stated that I was Coach 3, seat D13. Unlucky for some? An unwanted omen maybe? No. I don't believe it. Life is what you make it.

As we drew away from the station I whispered determinedly "No going back now Leah. You are on your way."

My longstanding relationship with Dan was over. At the age of 27 we had been together for four years. We had had a ball! Our interests were similar, both enjoying travelling, the gym, walking, dancing and socialising with friends. Quite a broad range of interests that had taken us out and about the North East of England, having fun together. We had met on the dance floor both gyrating at a nightclub. Our eyes met when he meekly said "Let's dance" He was a fantastic dancer, probably his greatest gift and made it all look so easy. I was immediately attracted to him. He had a nice face and a hunky slim body. Dan had learnt to dance from childhood and it showed. Over our time together I found him to be funny with a placid nature, sometimes a bit too placid as it turned out.

Dan, a qualified electrician, was an only child with a rather overbearing mother. Sweet as she was on first acquaintance I found Sue to be a strong character that you wouldn't cross lightly. She showed what she was thinking but didn't realise this trait in herself. I got to realise that she would turn a raging red from the neck upwards when something happened that prickled her, thus warning me to be careful! She wasn't the kind of woman to fall out with.

Dan never ever challenged his Mum. In my opinion he was unfortunately under her thumb. He even seemed to enjoy being ordered about by the strong woman that his mother was. That was the worrying part.

Our relationship had been a love at first sight romance. We sent sloppy cards on birthdays, ate candlelit dinners together in nice restaurants and exchanged expensive gifts. "I love you Leah" he'd say at least twice on every date. After the first two years it crossed my mind that this relationship was going nowhere. The cards grew smaller, the dinners less frequent and the presents became few and far between. It was however a comfortable relationship when just the two of us were together and I was busy working and studying so mistakenly just let it drag on.

Finally after four years I suddenly woke up. The strong woman in me rose to see this was a failing connection with the wrong person. I was wanting more from our relationship but Dan was so unable to commit as he was too strongly influenced by his mother. She would make unnecessary comments like 'You don't want to get tied up with a mortgage' or 'Best to stay single as long as you can.' Not exactly helping matters and making me wonder if I wanted a Mother-in-Law like her in my life.

All the things that a girl expects from a four year relationship were never mentioned. A longed for surprise, romantic proposal, a sparkling diamond engagement ring, a fabulous wedding, a princess gown to wear down the aisle and a champagne reception in a fabulous country house. These proved to be just a romantic wish list.

I was not set totally on that route. As a modern woman I would have been happy to simply set up a cosy warm home, sharing long winter nights snuggling up together with a takeaway and a good film on Netflix. We would have managed nicely without interference from Dan's mother.

It dawned on me that Dan couldn't face up to the realities of life like rent, bills and the possibility of a family. Moving on and taking chances, like most young people was certainly not part of Dan's agenda...... his mother's influence had bitten!

I wasn't going to ruin my life waiting for something that was never going to happen so bravely, I ditched Dan.

I had a great friend from school who knew Dan. Her name was Lynne. She had been by my side through all the ups and downs and I respected her outlook on life.

"Destiny, Leah, Destiny." she always said as if it was the answer to everything.

Lynne was a strange young woman, apparently named after a cascade from the top of Mount Everest and her middle name was genuinely Destiny. She came from a free spirited family. Her Granny had been a hippy and had spent several years living in a commune. Her mother had a tinge of free spirit in her and earned her living teaching belly dancing in Adult Education. Surprisingly enough Lynne was quite the opposite. As a teenager she had been cautious and sensible for a young person. Lynne wouldn't touch alcohol, pick up a boyfriend from the dancehall or eat out. However she was a good friend to me and had helped me over lots of issues, especially when my Dad died. "Your life is already planned. Nothing you do will change its course " Lynne told me."Just go with the flow."

I really saw the light regarding Dan when we had been on our first mini cruise together. There was Dan, of course his mother Sue had to come too ....and me! We went to Bruges and Amsterdam on a wonderful glamorous ship. The facilities were out of this world. "Its like a huge floating hotel" I cried excitedly. There were glass lifts looking down onto a sunken atrium, a cocktail bar with a pianist softly setting the romantic mood and restaurants with waiters industriously serving delicious food and giving top class service. The large plush theatre was opulent, like the big theatres in Blackpool. The casino was full of optimistic punters hoping for a win at the gaming tables.

There was a choice of swimming pools and dancing venues.

Our all-inclusive drinks package provided cocktails until the early hours complementing the excitement of the late night Disco. As if that wasn't enough there was a daily programme of fun things on offer and the opportunities of seeing the highlights of Amsterdam and Bruges once we had docked.

It could have been brilliant but in her annoying way Sue spoilt it for me.

I hadn't been away for ages and I was completely exhausted from the demands of studying on my days off and holding down a full time nursing job. I just needed a rest and a change and this short break would have been more than sufficient. Sue was a regular cruiser and didn't she let me know it!

At every opportunity Sue tried to put me down with her knowledge of cruise procedures, like the imminent safety briefing and the swipe card used to get into your room or pay for your purchases. " You don't both need your swipe card with you all the time." she said. Of course she was wrong as I found out when I was separated from Dan, couldn't find him and so was stranded outside my room after unsuccessfully looking for him on a ship carrying 2000 people. "Leah," I said to myself. "Don't let her get to you"

One legal requirement is to attend a safety briefing. I had a wry smile on my face when at the briefing Sue tried to put on her life-jacket and got in an absolute muddle with the Velcro fastening, the long dangling straps and even the way round the lifejacket had to go." Just copy me" she said. She knew best! Even though she didn't.

Here are some examples of the irritating nonsense that I had to put up with. How I kept my temper I'll never know. Every morning Sue would tell Dan what he should eat for breakfast. "Special K isn't so fattening "Dan, you can have that" she said in her ordering tone. "You don't want to spoil your lovely waistline." Once he had eaten his Special K she told Dan that he shouldn't eat the cooked breakfast as it was too fattening.

Sue suggested that Dan shouldn't shave for the duration of the mini cruise as she wanted to see what he would look like.

She thought and hoped that he'd resemble Nick Knowles, the TV presenter of whom she was a fan.

Naturally Dan did what he was told and just looked scruffy. Not once did he stand up to his mother but I took it all in and remembered every order and command, mentally planning how I was to end this dead end relationship.

Sue said I should encourage Dan to go to the ship's gym twice a day even though I'd said that we would miss the early evening show in the ship's theatre.

She told Dan what shirt to wear for dinner and even came into our room to choose his socks! I found her attitude and meddling manner unacceptable.

Luckily we were only away for four nights so I tried to bite my tongue. "It wont be for much longer." I told myself. I had seen the light! Plans for the break up with Dan were consolidating in my head during this trip.

I wrangled with my feelings and decided to just live with it as this relationship is going under like a ship sinking!

Imagine this woman being your Mother-in-Law. You'd have no peace. She would be telling me what to buy for dinner, how to do the washing and how to keep a clean home. The words 'Control Freak' came to mind. She was full of her own self importance and didn't appear to have any empathy towards anyone. "Don't do it that way. Do it this way" were some of her common phrases.

I tried to hide my feelings from Dan but it was hard to keep smiling. In any case, he seemed oblivious that anything was wrong.

Looking back I should have challenged Sue for her attitude and interfering ways, especially as I am a strong woman and don't usually put up with nonsense.

Once back home I met Dan for what he expected to be a usual night out and plucked up the courage to tell him that our relationship was at an end.

I struggled emotionally to find the right choice of words, not wanting to appear callous and uncaring. Four years together was not to be sniffed at. In the end I grabbed the bull by the horns and just blurted it out. "Dan, our lives are going nowhere and I want to finish our relationship."

Once said I felt pleased with myself that I wasn't letting Sue or Dan spoil my life. This news obviously came as a complete shock. Dan was visibly shaking, pale and speechless. I tried to be kind but when you finish any long-standing relationship it is cruel. It was however, necessary.

I walked back to my car staring at the ground and in a stunned state. I had mixed and muddled feelings. The loss of a friend, companion and partner was combining with thoughts of new freedom and opportunity. I sat quietly in my car for a few minutes reflecting on our meeting before driving home with a sense of overall relief. I had done the right thing.

A week later the 'phone rang at home. Interfering Sue had the cheek to call my Mum and complain that I had upset her son. "Lucky escape," I said to myself. Lynne was right. Destiny and my own common sense had played a part.

I continued my journey down to London listening to the strong beat of Bob Marley on my iphone. It was familiar music. I smiled to myself and took strength from the words of the song 'Don't worry about a thing, cos every little things gonna be alright.'

I looked around the carriage at the other passengers and wondered where their journeys would take them. The sad, tired looking man working industriously on his laptop, the harassed mother with a sweet three year old little girl and the teenage girl with a worried look. I wondered if anyone in that carriage was also on the verge of a new life.

I knew it was going to feel strange in new surroundings and not having Dan around as we had got so used to each other, but familiarity breeds contempt.

I was somewhat drawn by the excitement of a strange vibrant city and a sense of fulfilment in having made such a big leap. I was determined to succeed and make my mark. Where better than London for a fresh start?

The train glided into Euston Station and I took one deep

breath. "Leah Harris, you have made it" I murmured. "My new life starts from now"......

CHAPTER 3

New beginnings

Mum had given me her full support to see a bit more of the world and to get away from my hometown. She agreed that I needed a change, a new start and a chance to recover away from my Blackpool. I was a bit concerned to leave as Mum was widowed but she assured me that she was independent, in good health and young for her years. She had a wide circle of friends and as she said with the aid of modern technology we could keep in touch easily. Facetime, Facebook, emails and mobile 'phone all made keeping close to Mum so easy. "We can catch up on the gossip and banter easily on Skype." Mum had said.

Mum's exact words I shall never forget. "Leah, I want the best for you and staying in Blackpool isn't right for you just now. Go and see a bit more of the world. You have worked so hard to get your nursing qualifications so see where they take you."
Mum was such a sensible woman. I trusted every bit of advice that she gave me. She had been rocked by the early death of my father but had valiantly rallied round, made a new life for herself and got on with it. Such strength.

As an only child some Mum's would have hung onto their only daughter but my Mum had visions of a new and exciting future for me. "You can be down in London in less than three hours these days." she said. So with new vigour and determination I had booked my ticket and planned my future.
Through sheer hard work and dogged determination I had

gained my degree and Nursing and Midwifery Council certificate, which had taken me a challenging three years. Burning the midnight oil, plus early rising to study and the support from my Mum had all contributed to my achievement. Although exhausted it had been worth it. Feeling proud I was now a Registered Nurse.

I followed with a year's work on an orthopaedic ward which was a great experience. I loved the patients, their warmth and banter. Their broken bones, trauma and shock could never strip them of their senses of humour.

Taking the Nursing adults route involved 50% practical nursing and 50% placements in health care and community settings. At times complete exhaustion had preyed on me with the idea of giving up but my sense of commitment to become a nurse had ruled over me. 'It's only another year' I convinced myself. Fortunately having got so far had enabled me to reason with myself to carry on and finish. The reward was that I was the first person from my family to go down the nursing route.

Mum was proud of me and that made me feel good. I'd never let her down..

How some of the others on the course managed I shall never know. On top of the demands of the course they had young families to cope with adding to their stress.

My nursing training would stand me in good stead. With a job lined up through an nursing agency, at a top London hospital, well, I can't go wrong. That is what I told myself. 'Who knows what might evolve. The world is my oyster. You only have one life so live it to the full.'

So with all that behind me I had arrived at bustling Euston Station. I walked through the overcrowded concourse. People from all corners of the world were there, many transfixed to the Arrivals and Departures board awaiting further news before rushing off to their platform. I felt small and insignificant as I scurried across the public space heading eagerly towards an empty seat.

Sitting for a while I watched the world go by and composed myself. There was a lot to take in. "London at last" I murmured. "Pull yourself together Leah, you can do it."

On the verge of losing confidence I took long deep breaths to help to calm me down. Panic could so easily have taken over but the deep breaths soon got me back
on an even keel..
I spent a good twenty minutes coming to terms and reflecting on where I was, what I was doing and why I was doing it. The situation was daunting but I was 'going for it'. A new job, a new home and new opportunities.

The Internet had given me the necessary information for my onward journey so reaching for my hand written notes I found myself on the deep Northern line of the London Underground

Everywhere was so busy with people rushing in all directions with their busy commitments and lifestyles. The platform was packed six deep with visitors and workers of all nationalities making their journeys near and far. It was a hot summer evening and I felt clammy gasping for the need for fresh air. The tube train was heaving as it was that time of day that many were re-turning home after work. Not a seat in sight and me here, block-ing the gangway with my heavy suitcase, feeling embarrassed.

I looked around me and saw many others in a similar situ-ation. It is all part of living in a big city I thought. Nobody takes any notice. Nobody speaks and nobody makes eye contact. I needed to get used to this kind of behaviour which appears to be the norm. A far cry from the friendly Northerners that I was used to.......

I was heading for Camberwell, South London where I had managed to find a house-share with four other people. It was a large three storey Victorian house which I found through a won-derful online site called Gumtree.

I had scoured Gumtree relentlessly looking for somewhere affordable and suitable. Rents in London are ridicilously high.

"That one sounds quite nice." Mum had said. "You won't know what its like until you live there. It's all pot luck." she said.

This particular house share was quite near to my new job so I could save on fares. A nurses wages are not that great and the cost of living in London was expensive. Every penny saved would help.

So trundling along with a sense of trepidation, my heavy suit-case filled to bursting with clothes; a photo of Mum, my laptop, bed linen, my address-book and best make up, I continued my journey.

Finding the house was easy. I gingerly knocked on the front door with the original heavy iron door knocker. I could hear laughter coming through the door and I remember thinking that this was a good sign. The door opened and a smiling young woman opened the door.

" Hi." she said. "You must be Leah. We had been wondering what time you would turn up. Welcome to London. My name is Jessica. Come on in. You must be worn out after your journey. I'll make you a cuppa. Tea or coffee? Then I'll introduce you to the other housemates."

"Hi, yes I'm Leah. Lovely to meet you. Tea please. You can't beat a good brew after a long journey. Thank you so much" I replied.
Jessica looked about the same age as me and immediately I felt that we would get along. She had flowing corkscrew curls and a big smile.

Next I was introduced to Ellen, a very pretty young woman with brilliant blue eyes and a soft Irish accent. "Love your ac-cent. Ellen. Where do you come from?" She told me that she came from Waterford in Ireland and was a nurse like me.

Phil, the only man of the house, was in the sitting room with his Beats on his ears listening to his music. He was older and looked quite stern. Ellen explained that he worked long hours in the music industry.

Phil was the 'manager' of the house and it was to him that we would be answerable and pay our monthly rent to. I won't be upsetting him by paying the rent late, I thought.

I was told that Jasmine also shared the house. She worked in Retail and was at work but I would meet her soon. She had only recently joined the house and had come from Singapore.

Phil, having been disturbed from his music, rather begrudgingly showed me to my room and explained a few of the do's and don'ts of the house. Once alone his manner softened slightly and I thought that maybe he would be alright after all. Still, better keep on the right side of him. "Thank you for your help Phil " I said gratefully.

My room was larger than I had expected and was on the first floor. It was clean and pleasantly decorated and the double bed felt comfy. I sat on the edge of the bed and took in the surroundings. The house had a nice feel and I felt comforted. I unpacked my suitcase and hung up my clothes, filled the chest of drawers and pushed the suitcase under the bed. Luckily there was a little desk and chair where I could plug in my laptop computer so I could send emails and use the Internet. Better let Mum know I have arrived.

'Hi Mum,' I wrote 'Journey went well. All good here. Found the house OK. Housemates are friendly and welcoming. Think I'm going to like it.. Worn out. Speak tmoz. Love you, Leah'

Wearily I made the bed up with the new duvet set from home and plumped up the pillows. Mum wasn't behind me picking my things off the floor anymore so best to keep it all shipshape, I told myself.

I went downstairs to find that Ellen had made me a delicious toastie and another cuppa! "Aww. Thanks for making me so welcome everyone. I think I will be very happy here." I settled in, did a lot more chatting and getting to know the housemates, with a bit of TV now and then before deciding on an early night. I could have slept on a plank of wood if I had to. It had been an exceptionally busy day.

I said a little 'Thank you' to Him up there! This was quite an unusual thing for me to do but I felt it was well deserved.

That night I fell into a cosy, deep sleep, grateful that everything had gone well. So far so good.

CHAPTER 4

New job and new boyfriends

As I had specialised as an Orthopaedic nurse my new position was in a similar vein. My hospital was large and it was difficult to find my way around. The winding corridors, lifts, staircases, signs and notices were everywhere. Compared to my Blackpool hospital it was massive. Would I ever crack it? There was so much to learn.

The hospital was moved from the centre of London to its current site in 1909. It had begun as a small hospital and buildings had been added over the years. These were a variety of architectural styles, ranging from the original Edwardian main building down to clinics held in modern portacabins-all relevant and needed. To this day the hospital has grown to serve 700,000 inner city people and is a referral centre for some medical specialisms.

Everywhere I went I saw people, people and more people. Some were staff from operating theatres with their blue headgear, uniforms and comfy theatre shoes and others wearing well pressed shirt, tight fashionable trousers and stethoscopes. These were the Doctors, often males, looking quite young and in most cases very handsome. Maybe there would be one for me! There were radiographers, occupational therapists, physiotherapists, psychologists, healthcare assistants, pharmacists and volunteers amongst others all, buzzing about going on their daily shifts. Of course there were also countless members of the public coming throughout the day for appointments or to visit friends and family.

I spent an essential training day undertaking an Induction programme to learn about the hospital Trust policies and procedures and of course the obligatory Health and Safety procedures. I found this a great opportunity to mingle with other new staff members in the same position as me. I met with my new line manager and was told of the hospital buddy scheme, the evaluation of my work at an annual appraisal, job shadowing and professional development. It was a lot to take in. I was absolutely bursting with information, do's and don'ts, new faces, new surroundings and lots of names of clinics, theatres and wards. Who knows where this London life might lead! I began to feel a bit smug at having made this brave step.

I decided that I needed a fresh London look to go with my new job. After catching sight of myself in the long mirror by my bed, I could see that I needed to trim up and to lose weight. I vowed to do more exercise. So cutting out pies, cakes and biscuits and forcing myself to go for a jog around the block once a day, I soon rediscovered my slim waist and toned body.

Fortunately I had inherited my fathers wavy hair but it was a bit of a dowdy colour shade of nothing. Highlights would be the answer, I thought, so once I had received my first payday, I took myself on an expensive visit to the hairdressers and came out a different person!

As a busy nurse I found that just a touch of bright lipstick lit up my face and made a huge difference so promised myself to regularly top up as necessary. I was happy with the result of my new regime. Although I looked date perfect I had done this for myself, my health and to make the most of being in my twenties. After all this time in my life would never come round again.

Sam worked at the hospital in Security. I'd spotted him in the hospital shop getting a coffee and had thought that he looked well toned. He was tall, dark and handsome but didn't he know it! We went to the cinema for our first date. The second date was ten pin bowling where he won hands down and the third was a quiet chat at a pub which was my choice. Sam was younger than me and it showed. He was a macho man, full of himself and his big muscles and as I soon discovered was not my type at all. At the pub, after listening to a long reveal about how he had got right up to someone's face, making them back off, I saw the light. He said he'd pick me up on Friday night but I replied convincingly "Sorry Sam, unfortunately I can't make it as I am studying." It was a white lie but I had to get him off my back. When he next called me I was again up to my eyes studying! Only a few days later I spied Sam with his hand on the wall as if preventing a young pretty nurse from getting away. I heard him say " Come on beautiful. Who can refuse a date with someone as good looking as me." That was the end of Sam.

I rang to tell Lynne who as usual said "It's in the stars Leah. It's all planned already. No, Sam wasn't the one for you. You deserve better. He will come. Wait and see. You will meet your destiny when the time is right" She added, "You know Leah, I'm very envious of you going to London and having all this excitement. I'm stuck here in a dead-end job waiting for what's in the stars for me."

Trying to urge Lynne to do something about her boring life I spoke to her honestly. "Everyone gets chances in life. It is how you use your chances that count. If you are in a dead end job for goodness sake do something about it!" I hoped that she would think about my words of advice.

The next date for me came along quickly after Sam. We met in the local Library over the photocopier where I had gone for a copy of my signed rental agreement. We stood there and chatted informally for a while. Henry was a Londoner, born and bred. He was of the more mature type with a sallow skin and dark beard. His dress style was casual, jeans and a check shirt that looked like it needed to see the iron, however he seemed nice enough. When he asked me for a date I agreed. Being wary of meeting someone that I didn't know in their home I suggested that we should go to a Museum. I said that the Victoria and Albert Museum would be good. Instead Henry arranged for us to meet at the Imperial War Museum for our first date. Not exactly a romantic environment but all credit to the museum staff, the exhibitions were amazing and the cafe was good. We got on well at first but as we got to know each other better I began to see the flaws. It turned out that Henry was the exact opposite to Sam. He was too gentle for me, too sensitive but in the wrong way. In fact you could call him a wimp! He talked a lot about his indigestion, his food allergies, hay fever and his gluten free diet. I heard about his irritable bowels, his migraine headaches and his dodgy hip. HELP, I thought. All he wants is a nurse and it's not going to be me. I didn't want to cause him more medical problems with our break-up, like nervous tension, sleepless nights and anxiety so my little white lie came in useful again. My regular excuse was "I'm studying so can't make it. Sorry." After several attempts to meet up he went away.

The following boyfriend was sweet but another who was under his mother's thumb. 'How do I attract these weak men' I thought. At twenty nine he lived at home with his elderly mum and was just too pampered. She would wake him up for work, bring him tea in bed and lay out his clothes for the morning. She generally spoilt him and he loved it. Luckily he was moving to Somerset with his Mum who wanted to retire near the sea."You must come and visit me" he said. 'Not on your life I thought.'

CHAPTER 5

A tug at the heart strings

So my new London life had begun and got off to a flying start. I am so busy on the ward rushing about, changing dressings, communicating with patients and team members, giving medication and completing patient records, not forgetting the touch of promised lipstick as needed. Luckily I'm in a great team on an orthopaedic male ward with a diverse range of patients of all ages, races and backgrounds. I love the patients. They keep me going and are always laughing and joking. I have to liaise with lots of people, not only the patients but also their families. It is interesting and rewarding work.

I am loving London but occasionally, when I get a minute I think about the green rolling hills and fields bordering Blackpool, the villages and the warm friendly people with their northern accent. It is very different here. I think of the friends that I have left behind there and just occasionally have a little pang of emptiness but I quickly pull myself up and move on with my thoughts as I want to make a success of this new experience.

With some surprise I had a Facebook message from Dan, my ex. boyfriend in Blackpool. He said that he had time to think things over and now realised that he needed to be stronger and stand up to his mother.
'Too bad 'I thought. 'Too little, too late. You had your chance and blew it.' I didn't want to be unkind so I replied that I was enjoying my new life and had been lucky to find a super shared house and that I hoped that he and his mother were keeping well!

Again I called Lynne. I wanted to tell her that Dan had tried to make contact, especially as she knew every detail of my broken romance off by heart, inside out and from start to finish. In fact, I had gone on about Dan and his mother so much that Lynne must have been sick of hearing about it.

"Leah, You know that his mother was the fly in the ointment and you know how boys get hung up about their mothers. RUN, LEAH, RUN.

"Thanks Lynne. You are right." I said. "I am about to run the four minute mile."

That weekend Ellen from my house and I decided to go out. We were both at the same hospital but on different wards. Luckily our shift patterns were very similar and we felt like spoiling ourselves after the trials of a busy working week.
We spent Saturday afternoon getting ourselves ready with a pampering afternoon. The tweezers for tidying our eyebrows, the nail file and polish, the tinted foundation cream, the long length mascara and a host of different lipsticks adorned the dressing table. The heated brush, rollers and hairspray completed the array as we made ourselves beautiful! It was fun. Ellen and I shared the same sense of humour and we both felt like we had known each other for years. We had so much in common. "This is great" Ellen said. "Seems ages since I did anything like this. In fact I had forgotten what fun it is to make up and what a difference a splodge of colour on the cheeks and a whiff of perfume can do to the way you feel." I helped Ellen with her hair and she painted my fingernails a racy red. We put on our best and most fashionable outfits with our highest heeled shoes and with a squirt of perfume set off.

Looking far more glamorous than ever we went for a comedy night in Bloomsbury. It was a plush venue and we soon settled in expecting a super evening, probably helped by the gin and the cocktails that we were drinking. "This is what I have missing from my life. Can't we do this more often?" Ellen said with a slightly slurred tone. "Yep, we must make the effort, otherwise we will turn into a pair of sad old spinsters." I replied.

The show was amazing. We chuckled at the brilliant stand-up comedians. Our mascara and liner ran down our cheeks from laughing at the fast delivery of the endless jokes. "Such talent. How on earth do they remember it all" I said. "I'm not sure if the drink is making me laugh or the comedian" said Ellen "What is more I don't even care."
After the show we had a meal and while dining Ellen opened her heart up to me and told me of her background in her beloved Ireland. She told me of her family, about her sisters, her funny teasing father and her loving mother who was the heart of her family who just couldn't do enough for her girls. It was lovely to hear and I told her of my own strong sensible loving mother and the happy childhood that she had given me.

Coincidentally Ellen had been in a long-standing relationship but with an older man called Patrick. He was divorced but just like my ex. Dan, he too was afraid to commit to moving their relationship forward. Ellen felt strongly that the failure of his first marriage had been too much for him. "I suppose you could be right " I said. "Men are not always as tough as they make out, plus some women can be spiteful and cruel. One never quite knows what goes on behind closed doors." Ellen agreed but added that she loved Patrick deeply but wasn't going to waste her child-bearing years. "One day, Leah, I want a family of my own and I don't think I'd achieve that by staying with Patrick."

That is how Ellen had ended up in London. She had dug her heels in, upped sticks and left Ireland and her folks, taking her broken heart with her to search for comfort and a loving relationship in a new life.

Probably not helped by the drinking of gin and cocktails, Ellen became melancholic and tears began to flow. I tried hard to comfort her but she was inconsolable. I completely understood Ellen's feelings and how she was missing the warmth of the Irish, the comfort of her mother, the banter and all that goes with being in a loving family and of course reluctant Patrick. It was how I felt now and then, only for me it was my hometown, Blackpool, my mother and friends.

We decided to make our way home. We were both a bit the worst for wear and vowed not to drink gin in the future. Our feet were killing us and we ended up carrying our heels as we hobbled barefoot from the bus-stop home.

Before going to sleep I reflected on our day out. It had begun with such fun and laughter and ended on a sad note. But no, I wasn't going to let any emotions affect my time in London. I had made a great friendship with Ellen and we had got on so well. I felt that we had the world at our feet and time would be a healer for us both.

Get behind us Patrick and Dan

CHAPTER 6

Autumn comes and so does a cold

It is now autumn and the trees are almost bare. As I walk to work in the damp air I take special care not to slip as it is wet underfoot and fallen leaves are treacherous. I don't want to be a casualty statistic at my own hospital!

I love the spring and summer months most of all and never want them to end but nothing can stop nature and the world's natural clock giving us the seasons.

Just before Christmas there is the Winter Solstice when we have the shortest day in the northern hemisphere. After that each day gets a little lighter gradually as it moves towards the longest day on 21st June. Can't wait for that. It doesn't get dark until around 10pm.

The clock went back an hour last weekend and is now officially on Greenwich Mean Time. At 4pm it begins to get dark and it feels creepier when you are in unfamiliar surroundings. "It doesn't last forever" Ellen said optimistically. Ellen wasn't so keen on the dark evenings either - the pair of us not being used to such a big imposing capital city.

It is so cold in the mornings and the radiator in my room is fairly useless but I soldier on. Must report that radiator to Phil, my housemate. We barely meet due to my shifts and him being a quiet private soul, keeping himself to himself.

At work we have been given the opportunity for the flu jab but being rushed off my feet I didn't manage to make my slot last Monday. I regret this as now I am feeling sniffy and shivery. Whether or not it is flu I don't know so at home I make myself a hot medication lemon drink and take to my bed.

Ellen checked on me. "Anything I can get you Leah?" "No I'm

fine. Wish I'd had that flu jab though. One reason for missing it is because I'm scared of needles." "Be gone with you Leah" Ellen said in her no nonsense Irish accent. "You a nurse and you're scared of needles." Roaring with laughter she went back downstairs.

Where the next 4 hours went to I do not know. I was awoken by a phone call on my mobile. It was Mum worried that she hadn't heard from me. We often have a video call but I have just been completely zonked out so haven't been in touch.
"Good job it is my time off so I am not letting anyone down at work, though I can't see myself going in to work in two days time if I'm like this." I told her. I reassured Mum that I would live to tell the tale then got back into bed and drifted off again.
Hours later, in fact the next morning, feeling a little brighter and that the worst of the cold was over I was woken up by the slamming of the heavy front door. I kept a keen ear out as I didn't know who was in the house. Soon I heard talking and realised it was Phil, the guy who lives here and manages our house, having a 'phone conversation.

When Phil had finished on his 'phone I called out to him to let him know that I was at home. I presumed that he hadn't expected to find me in.

Phil came upstairs and asked if it was alright to come in. I was a little surprised so rearranged myself quickly, hiding the numerous tissues under my pillow. I tried hard to look presentable in my PJ's with a bright red and sore nose. "Are you sure that you want to come in here" I said croakily. "I don't want to give this bug to you." "No worries" replied Phil. He explained that he had left work early to collect a parcel from the Post Office.... something important that he had bought online.
Phil sat on the chair in my room and for the next hour we chatted away. We talked about missing our hometowns and the difficulties we had found when we first came to London. "I got muddled with the bus routes getting a 68 when it should have

been a 468 so I got completely lost." "Oh no. A similar thing happened to me." I said. "And the trains, they go here there and everywhere. It's so confusing. "We laughed about coincidences and misunderstandings. The chat had brought me back into the real world and I was now feeling a lot better.

Phil went on to tell me that job opportunities in the music industry had brought him to London twelve years ago. He had lived in a little village called Cross in Hand which was not so far from Eastbourne on the south coast. Phil smiled fondly as he recalled his village."It has a petrol station, a motorcycle shop, a bakery, a funeral director's, a parish church and one pub! A far cry from London." he reminisced."It is a beautiful area, so peaceful." he said. His village facilities also included a rugby club and it was through belonging that Phil had managed to get to know 'a weekender' high up in the music industry. The aqauintance had offered Phil a start in the industry, following his degree in Music Technology at the University of Sussex. Now, twelve years on Phil had worked his way up to become a Live Sound Crew Coordinator. It all sounded very new and unfamiliar to me. Phil had to hire people in line with business needs and keep within stipulated budgets. He said that he was finding it very stressful and sometimes yearned for his old village life and that his job wasn't so exciting now, in fact he was bored. "There must be more to a working life that this" he said."What I need is a proper career path." Chatting to Phil seemed comfortable and I liked his soft kindness.

Phil kindly made me another drink and brought me up a fresh hot water bottle.
One conversation led to another and we decided that when I was back to full strength and our work didn't clash we would take a day out to visit the countryside to get back that feeling of wide open spaces and the sky above us. We we obviously not true 'townies' yet.
I snuggled back down into my bed and with these plans in my mind I recalled the country walks that I used to take and how I

loved the countryside in all its seasons. In particular, I loved the area called the Ribble Valley, with its dry stone walls, railway viaduct and meandering river. The coastline around Blackpool was amazing. I recalled walking barefoot along the beach at Morcambe Bay and sitting, watching the sun drop into the sea.

Probably because I wasn't well I felt a bit lost and out of my depth. I need to get my strength back, soldier on and enjoy my new London life to the full .

CHAPTER 7

A complete change

So it was after Christmas, in fact mid January before Phil and I managed to book a day out together to the countryside. "Against the odds we have made today happen." I nodded in agreement. Phil continued. "We lead such busy and fast lives that sometimes we have to say stop, look around, take in the moment and enjoy." How right he was.

We took an early train to Westhumble Station by Box Hill, for a complete change of scenery. It was a surprisingly short journey. Arriving at the station it seemed peaceful and the fresh country air was welcome.
Just a couple of passengers got off the train. They were met by friends or relatives. "No line of red London buses here. People have to rely on friends, family or their two flat feet." Phil remarked.

We walked to the end of the road past smart family homes that were tucked away and finally came to a wide main road with noisy cars and lorries and the familiar stench of diesel. "I thought we had come to the country" I said to Phil. "Trust me." he smiled as he knew that once we had got past the busy road we would find the peace and tranquillity that we were looking for. "Look ahead. There is Box Hill. We are going right to the top. We can get across this busy road by the underpass."
A hard to find gate took us to a wide open field. We took the footpath with the River Mole to our left. Chatting away we noticed the recent rain and snow had made the river swollen and fast running. A rope swing had been abandoned but you could imagine the fun children would have swinging on the rope in the sunshine and the families picnicking, enjoying special time together. The noise from the traffic was now no more than a dis-

tant hum. "What a lovely spot and so close to London." I said.

Now we were the only souls around, braving the chilly wind. It was cold but the sky was bright and it felt good to breathe in the chilled fresh air.

Phil and I had both dressed appropriately in walking boots, waterproof, windproof jackets with plenty of layers underneath. I certainly didn't look my most glamorous but Phil wasn't the kind of guy to notice. He looked rugged and his red puffa jacket and navy cord trousers suited his casual style. We had never discussed his age but I suspected that he was quite a lot older than he looked.

We crossed a bridge that took us to the base of Box Hill. Phil pointed out a river crossing that was submerged under the stream. "This is where there are stepping stones. In fact the crossing is called The Stepping Stones. In summer you can walk across the river on the stones. There are always lots of people at the weekends round this part having fun, children paddling and splashing about ..... weather permitting, of course."
We began our stiff climb to the top of Box Hill. It was wet, slippery and muddy underfoot. Phil was a good strong walker but it had been too long since I climbed a hill so was a bit out of practice. I found the ascent challenging! There were steps for most of the way which helped. Half way up I had to stop to catch my breath. It was then that Phil helped to haul me up the slippery path. Phil would have been much quicker without me but he didn't leave my side, being a perfect gentleman.

So resting a while, on a well-placed seat, we admired the view across from the North Surrey Downs. The cutting wind made it too cold to sit for long. "Come on Leah" said Phil. "You'll get cold if you sit for too long. Race you to the top." So laughing I tried my best to run uphill for the last leg of the ascent but as you may guess Phil made it first.
At the top we shared a view from Salomans, a newly refur-

bished viewpoint where we could see for miles. "The view must be stunning in the summer when the trees are out and everything is lush and green " I said. Phil nodded in agreement whilst taking in the wintry scene. Phil explained to me that Leopold Salomans, a wealthy London financier, had bought Box Hill to protect it from development. He had donated it to the National Trust years ago. Someone in Phil's distant family had been a great acquaintance of Leopold which is how Phil was so knowledgeable about the area. Phil said "Box Hill was named after the ancient Box trees and that there was a grave on the hill where a man had been buried head down!" "Really. Are you kidding me? This, I must see" I said. "It is absolutely true" Phil assured me. "The man was an eccentric. One explanation for his desire to be buried headfirst was that he thought the world was topsy turvy so he wanted to be buried that way!" "May he rest in peace!" I said.

After a delicious warming hot chocolate at the cafe and a mooch around the tempting National Trust shop we asked the sweet elderly assistant serving for directions to this strange burial site. We soon found the memorial stone on the west side of Box Hill. We read the stone with interest and Phil and I discussed how people with mental health issues might have been treated years ago. "Thank goodness there is better education about mental health nowadays" I said. That was the nurse in me coming out! "Yes, mental health is a terrible thing" Phil remarked with an understanding expression which made me wonder if he had experienced this himself.

We descended on the chalk face just as dusk was falling and wended our way to the pub near the station. Phil placed orders for a welcome meal and beers which were quickly delivered to our table. "This is so welcome but don't we just deserve it, after all that walking" I said, slowly sipping my beer. "You look like the fresh air has done you some good" said Phil. My cheeks were rosy from the wind and I was glowing. He looked rugged and strong as he picked up the glow of the nearby log fire.

This adventure into the countryside had been long overdue and it seemed that we had both benefitted from time out from work.
I looked at Phil. He was quiet, kind and caring. We had come out for the day as friends and we would now be going back home having got to know a lot more about each other, our interests, our pasts and our London lives.

We didn't discuss our friendship and whether it might become more than just friends, so it was just two friends for the time being. I did sense that there was a strange connection with Phil but not in a romantic sense. I just couldn't put my finger on quite what it was.

When I got back indoors I slipped into a hot bath and warm PJ's. Having recovered from the day I spoke to Mum for an hour, telling her of my wonderful day.

I Skyped Lynne to tell her all about Box Hill, with Phil. "We are just friends." I said. "What will be will be Leah" she said. "Your life is already planned. Time will tell. You need to believe."

CHAPTER 8

Mum visits and a chance meeting

Due to my shift pattern Mum and I hadn't managed to meet over Christmas, so Mum came to visit in late January.

"I'm really excited Leah. I haven't been to London for years and I'd love to see how it has changed. Last time I was there your father was working on a building development at the Museums" said Mum.

We'd Skype, sometimes for an hour. We'd discuss all the comings and goings in Blackpool, talking about news of our small family and what the two of us had been getting up to at work. Nothing however was as good as seeing my lovely Mum in the flesh. I felt really excited about her impending visit.
Mum had been quite a bit younger than my father. She used to tease him that he was a cradle snatcher. She was pregnant with me at the young age of nineteen. I think that I was a 'mistake' but that was never spoken about. If that was the case, I can guarantee that I was a love child. Mum and Dad were meant for each other, without a doubt.

When I lived at home I probably took Mum for granted. I didn't realise it at the time but she was always there for all the love and support I needed. I had a very happy childhood as both Mum and Dad made brilliant parents. I went to good schools, had lots of friends and probably accepted it all as being normal. Reflecting now, I can see that I was privileged in the way that I was given good values, a loving home and security.

Mum and Dad had lost a second baby who would have been my younger brother. It was never mentioned. I sensed it was too upsetting to talk about. I think it must have been a terrible shock as in the back of my mind I recall somebody telling me that the baby had died of an unexpected cot death. I can vaguely remember seeing my mother beside herself with grief when I was a very small child. In a bedroom drawer she keeps a tiny hand knitted pale blue set of tiny baby clothes. I suspect that she had made them for the son that didn't survive. I would have liked to have asked Mum but sensed that it was her undisclosed business, that she had wanted to keep it that way, close to her heart. So it remained her own private, sad secret.

Mums are wonderful human beings. I have observed a lot of deprivation, both in London and in Blackpool. Large families, often struggling in poor housing, with high rents and low wages. Despite these setbacks, mothers are doing their utmost for their families, ploughing on stoically, keeping children on the right path, feeding and nurturing them to the best of their abilities. The odds are against them but nothing deters their devotion. I have great admiration for these mothers and the way they are the backbone of their family, going without themselves for the sake of their children.

I have been so lucky. My Mum was really easy to get on with. It wasn't until I got to London that I reflected on our mother and daughter relationship, how supportive she had been over my broken romance with Dan and how I could open up and tell her everything.
What a beautiful woman she was in mind and body. If I could only be half a person as she was I'd be happy.

Mum was a lovely looking lady. She had a smooth unlined face with a strong bone structure emphasizing her high cheeks. Always a lovely warm smile, dark brown hair in an immaculate bob with attractive thick greying strands at the front. I know my Dad had loved every bone in her body. Mum missed him terribly yet kept a brave face. Life can be cruel when people are taken away from you. Bereavement changes so many lives in so many ways and there is no going back.

"Mum, when you hit London we are going to have brilliant time together." I promised, with a tone of excitement in my voice.
I was determined to make sure that Mum's visit was going to be one that she could look back on. I scoured the newspapers and Internet to see what was on so I could give Mum some choices and an action packed experience.
It was due to the forward planning and a bit of juggling that I had managed to get four consecutive days off.
I could really get to be a tourist myself, get to know London better and be with my lovely Mum.

Fortunately my housemate Jasmine had gone to see her family in Singapore as it was her special birthday. Jasmine was a sweet girl with perfect manners and an enviable head of shiny black hair that fell neatly to the back of her neck.
Out of fairness to Jasmine I rented her room for Mum's stay. Jasmine was lucky enough to have the only en-suite in the house, so I felt that I had a good result for making Mum's stay as luxurious and comfortable as possible. Jasmine's room was pretty with silky Sinhalese prints here and there, making it feel special. Jasmine had left the room in immaculate order and there was a welcome card in an envelope for Mum with a picture of a sunset on the front. So kind.... but that was Jasmine all over.
Well wrapped up I went to meet Mum off the train at Euston. I was lucky with connections and arrived far too early, for fear of being late. I sat on one of the few seats dotted about the station and began people watching, quite a favourite hobby of mine.

It was as busy in the daytime as on the evening that I had arrived. The station was buzzing. People rushing around some carrying hot and cold snacks, bottles of water and cans of drink for their journeys

'London's open!' I thought. Those words had been in the Mayor of London's recent campaign and it was true, every word. London would always be open to the world, open for business whilst celebrating inclusiveness and diversity.

While excitedly waiting for Mum's train to come in I got chatting to an immaculate, tall, slim older black man sitting next to me. He was extremely attractive with curling eyelashes and large brown eyes that were warm and welcoming. If only he was twenty years younger I thought. At first we chatted about the cold weather, being an easy topic for any conversation. Then gently questioning me asked "Do you work in London? Proudly I replied "Yes, I do. I am a nurse in an Orthopaedic ward. I trained in Blackpool and am now working at a large London hospital," He seemed impressed and nodded knowingly. "I have had a lot of experiences of hospitals in the past year or so as my elderly mother has been very ill but right now I'm just waiting for my train to go up to Liverpool for a business meeting." he said speaking softly with a beautiful strong scouse accent. He sounded just like the Beatles I thought. I loved his tone and accent. It was quite a different dialect from that of the Blackpool accent although the two towns were only sixty miles apart.

"I have lived in London, Brixton, south London to be precise, since coming down south fifteen years ago" he told me.

He went on to say that he was only going up for one night which was a pity as his family would hardly see him. He said that he would hope to make it to see his elderly Mum even for just an hour. "Pressures of London work mean I have to get back as soon as possible but I hope to snatch a week up there later in the year. I'll be able to spend some quality time and see my old Mum then."

Somehow we got chatting about how Liverpool was once the European Capital of Culture. As a teenager I had been there on a visit with my school. I recalled how we had gone to see wonderful production of A Midsummer's Night's Dream. We spoke about London and the array of theatrical productions on offer." I haven't made the most of the London shows because of the ticket prices which don't stretch on a nurses salary. What with the expense of living in rented property in London......." I confessed. "As a child I had loved ballet lessons and always imagined I'd be on the stage one day. Foolishly, as young people do, I gave it up. It is one of my big regrets. My only claim to fame is having taken part in the dancing school Christmas show. I think that I was about six years old." We laughed. "Oak trees from little acorns grow" said the stranger. "Bit late for that" I replied laughing.

My new acquaintance went on to ask me if I had ever been to see a live ballet. I told him that I hadn't yet but it would be something I would hope to do. Maybe with Mum one day. With that he whipped out his business card from a fine black leather holder and told me to give him a call in a day or so once he was back in London. He would like to arrange for Mum and I to go to see Matthew Bourne's production of Swan Lake at none other than the Sadler's Wells Theatre. The name on his card was Hilton Garrett. I was utterly taken aback but thanked him profusely and bid him a safe journey and to give my love to magical Liverpool. In a state of shock I read Mr. Garrett's business card and found that he was an artistic director of an arts company.

All too often we are untrusting and suspicious of strangers especially in big cities, yet my northern friendliness and life experiences must have struck a chord and it had paid off. I would certainly follow up his kind offer. Wow, that was an outcome.

In the distance between the rushing crowds I picked out the figure of Mum and very soon we were in each others arms.

CHAPTER 9

Time with Mum-our special day

Once we got back to the house we opened the street door to a lovely aroma of home cooking. Before meeting Mum I had a prepared a meal of Lancashire Hot Pot, just to make Mum feel at home. I had quickly got it together that morning and had left in slowly ticking over in the oven. It was piping hot and very welcome. The layers of potato were intertwined with lamb and onion, then cooked slowly in a large deep pot. I had made enough for the housemates too and on a chilly evening it was a big hit. Phil joined us at the table and with some steaming carrots and peas we all tucked in. We cracked open some wine and the conversation flowed. Mum and Phil chatted together like they had known each other for years. They seemed to have a lot in common liking the same kind of music, food and travel.

Next morning Mum and I decided to jump on one of the frequent and world famous red London buses and go shopping in Oxford Street. Once on the bus we chatted away and we got onto the subject of my recent unsuitable boyfriends. "Mum, I'm seriously looking for love." I said. "I'm at an age now when I would like to find someone to settle down with. Someone who I can share my life with. I seem to attract men but there is always some reason why the relationship ends. I have so much love to give so just need to find the right one." Mum replied. "Leah, you have plenty of time. Your recent dates just were not your type. You will find someone. I am a firm believer that there is someone out there for everyone. It just takes time.

Hasn't Lynne told you that your fortune is already planned for you?" "Yes, Lynne is always going on about my destiny." I laughed. I had expected this kind of response from Mum but thinking about it she was right and what more was there to say anyway?

We reached Marble Arch and went into all the department stores right to Oxford Circus.

Oxford Street is famous the world over. It can be found in the West End of London and attracts half a million visitors daily. In recent years other shopping centres have challenged the success of Oxford Street but for Mum and I there was nothing like it. We were like a couple of excited shopaholics.

In the space of two hours Mum had bought pastel blue matching shoes and bag to wear at a friends silver wedding party and some new undies. "Bit saucy Mum " I said laughing. "It's just this once." she replied.

I treated myself to a new wool jumper. Not much call for a huge wardrobe when you have to wear uniform for most of the time! "This will be useful and look good with my jeans" I said convincing myself that it was money well spent and a bargain.

At lunchtime we stopped off for a shared and welcome Margarita Pizza. It was a chance to rest our weary feet.
Rejuvenated by our lunch and glass of wine we strolled down Regent Street. We popped in and out of the exclusive shops, excited at the styles and ranges on offer. We admired the riot of colour portrayed in imaginative window displays. Fashion and fabrics displayed in fanciful ways. "Oxford Street and Regent Street windows take some beating." said Mum. "Yes," I replied. Even though people do Internet shopping there is nothing like the real thing. Feeling it, touching it and seeing it."

We warily crossed the roads at Piccadilly Circus trusting the green signals telling us when to cross. Traffic seemed to be coming from all directions. "Run. There's a taxi heading towards us!" I shouted to Mum. We safely reached the statue of Eros, the God of Love and carefully sitting on the steps spent a while resting and recovering. "He is what you need" said Mum, pointing to Eros. "Ask him to help!" We laughed as we picked ourselves up.

So now, with shopping over, I suggested that we made our way for afternoon tea. Little did Mum know that I had booked a superb, classic afternoon tea in a lavish boutique hotel at Victoria. Hope she can find space for it after all that pizza!.

The tea was a bit of a treat. I had hastily snatched a bargain offer on the Internet. It was soon to be Mum's birthday, so a one off luxurious experience was a good way to celebrate.

It started to rain. Luckily the 'phone app helped us locate the hotel. We have all this technology but it's easy to forget the help your mobile can give you. especially when you are out with your mum, having a great day, even in the rain! Luckily we were very close to the hotel and the app's directions were spot on. "There it is."I called as I spied the boutique hotel's sign. "Let's get inside before it pours down."

Anticipating a big treat we stepped into the plush Reception area, put the umbrella away in a brass stand and took off our jackets.

"Let me take those for you" said a smart young woman with an broken English accent. She checked our voucher and asked us if we were visitors to London. "I am" said Mum "but my daughter lives here.

" It seemed funny to hear this. I asked the lady what part of the world she had come from with her strong attractive accent. "I am from Budapest, Hungary" she said. "It is a beautiful city and has the river Danube running through it, like your Thames" she smiled. Wow, I thought and made a mental note to visit one day.

We took our places at the table. "This is very nice, look, proper tablecloths, starched and pure white" said Mum. "Real napkins and fresh flowers on the table. What luxury." She knew a thing or two about a quality afternoon tea, having spent some time working in the hospitality industry in Blackpool. The cups, saucers and tea plates were also to Mum's taste. Turquoise flowers with fine gold borders and the food was served on a three tiered afternoon tea stand.

The assortment of sandwiches were cut into neat fingers on the bottom tier. The middle tier held scones that were freshly baked and still warm. Separately in little pretty matching dishes was clotted cream and jam. The dainty cakes were beautiful creations and took the top tier of the cake stand. "This was living it up! Couldn't do this everyday." said Mum light-heartedly.

We munched through sandwiches and scones liberally topped with cream and jam and now it was the turn of the cakes. We could only manage a fresh cream éclair each and a tiny raspberry tart served in a sweet pastry but they were mouth watering and delicious. More piping hot tea was served on demand and we felt on top of the world. We sat back in the comfy chairs feeling very satisfied.

That was a glorious early birthday surprise for a special Mum. "Love you Mum" I said. "Love you too.

That was a wonderful treat." Mum added "There is nothing like a good English afternoon tea. Thank you."

All we could do now was to stagger back to the bus home feeling over full. "I couldn't manage another cake ever" I said.

Once indoors we collapsed onto the sofa and watched the television for the rest of the evening. It had been a great Mother and Daughter Day, a great rekindling experience. "Haven't we had a super day Mum? Time well spent catching up and reminiscing"
"I couldn't agree more Leah" smiled Mum.

CHAPTER 10

Following up with a phone call

Rather nervously I followed up with a phone call to the dark handsome man that I had chatted to on Euston Station. "Oh, Hi Mr Garrett" I said . "Do you remember me? We spoke at Euston Station and you asked me to call you when you were back in London. You said that you would arrange for my Mum and I to go to Sadler's Wells to see the ballet."

"Oh yes, of course I remember you" said Mr Garrett. "You are the nurse and you were waiting for your mother to arrive.

Yes, I have made the arrangements for you to see the ballet tomorrow evening, if that is convenient?"

"That's brilliant. Yes, tomorrow would work well. We would love to go. I can't thank you enough" I said in reply. "That is really kind of you. Is there anything I can do to repay your kindness?"

Mr Garrett advised me to go to the theatre and the Box Office would have an envelope for me.

He explained that his elderly mother had recently received such good treatment from the nurses while in a National Health Service hospital and that was his way of giving something back.

There was nothing I needed to do to repay him. What a lovely gesture and wasn't I so lucky to be the recipient?

That evening we enjoyed the most wonderful production of Swan Lake at Sadler's Wells Theatre.

"What a great seat. I can see the stage really well" said Mum.

The production was absolutely unbelievable with talented dancers twisting and turning in perfect unison in scene after scene. I envied the way they remembered every move, every gesture and every step.

"This is marvellous" whispered Mum.

The story was a spin on the traditional Russian ballet Swan Lake and featured a young Prince being taunted to join the swans. The costumes, scenery and effects were fabulous and imaginative. The swans, played by all male dancers, were powerful yet sensitive. There were comical touches, heaps of emotion and wonderment. This was complemented by the music which was beautiful. The sound of the live orchestra was a real treat and did justice to the music written by Tchaikovsky. I could recognise several of the pieces."This is my favourite piece from this ballet " whispered Mum." It was the finale, so powerful and moving that I felt tears run down my cheek and as I turned to Mum I could tell that she too was overcome, while loving every minute. "I could watch that all over again." she said fighting back her tears. "Absolutely wonderful and I think I can safely say it is the best thing I have ever seen on stage."
My words cannot do enough to tell of the beauty, power and originality of this production and the skills demonstrated by the dancers and musicians.

We travelled back to the house in silence, too stunned and overwhelmed to speak.

The ballet had a profound effect on me. I had enjoyed every minute and felt that the strong emotions it stirred inside me pinpointed what I wanted and needed in my life.

I needed to feel the power of love, be held in someone's strong arms, to be loved relentlessly, to feel wanted, adored, cherished, prized and treasured.

I wanted to find my own intense love with a new partner.

Where to look I do not know, but I do know now what I'm looking for.

That night I felt such admiration for Matthew Bourne and his artistic gift to bring such originality to a ballet.

The next day I wrote a 'Thank you' card to Mr Garratt for his kindness and the tickets. I especially mentioned his mother as it was because of her care from nurses when in a major Liverpool hospital that Mum and I had been the beneficiaries able see the ballet Swan Lake.There are still kind and generous people about.

I had a long phone chat with my friend Lynne, telling her about the emotions that I had experienced. "It is good that you have had these feelings so that you will recognise love when it comes along. It will happen. It's already planned." she said reassuringly

CHAPTER 11

Phil came too!

For Mum's last day in London she said that she would like to go to The Natural History Museum at South Kensington.

My late father had worked on the building many years ago as a plumber. Mum believed that it had been while working at the Museum he had contracted mesothelioma, a cancer linked with asbestos. Of course it was difficult to prove. Mum felt that a visit to the Museum would pay homage to my father.

Phil had asked Mum and I if he could join us. Since our day out to Box Hill I hadn't had much to do with Phil. We were both such busy people. "I'm at a loose end today as I'm on leave from work." Phil explained. "Of course you can" Mum said. She liked Phil. Off we set taking the red London double decker.
We had checked the current programmes on the Internet and chose to visit the Wildlife Photographer of the Year exhibition. One hundred winning and commended images were on show. Mum had always had a soft spot for wild animals so I knew she would find it enjoyable."Just look at those eyes" she said several times. "What a brilliant piece of photography. Just look at the way the light catches the animals fur." she wondered as she checked out the name of the photographer. Mum was really impressed by the quality and staging of the exhibition and it was just the kind of thing she enjoyed."This is a perfect day out. I'm loving it" She winked at me.

I had to agree that the wildlife photographs were amazing. They included insects, mammals and plants photographed with absolute clarity. Apparently the competition attracts fifty thousand entries from ninety two countries so you can imagine the quality of the works that get chosen. Mum said that she felt privileged to be able to see this amazing display. I felt the same way too.

We followed up by seeing the whales exhibition 'Beneath the Surface'. Again, totally amazing, breathtaking and wonderous. Phil loved this even more. "It's wonderful to give the public the opportunity to find out about these magnificent marine mammals" said Phil."We are so lucky with our Museums."

During our visit Phil didn't seem his usual self. He was very quiet. Maybe he was just tired. He seemed to have something on his mind but he was keeping it to himself. Despite this we went for lunch to a nearby Greek restaurant." My treat" said Phil."The food in here is really good" We dined on spit roasted meats, tzatziki and delicious pitta bread.
Over the meal Mum and Phil discussed the current political situation, the cost of living compared to the North and the benefits of living both in and out of London.They got on like a house on fire and Phil seemed to have cheered up a little.

Our next stop off was at the exquisite shop Harrods in Brompton Road, Knightsbridge. I had heard of Harrods but never had the opportunity to visit myself. I loved every minute of the experience being a shopaholic myself. I just wished that my salary could match the prices in the store.

From the outside you were immediately attracted by the stunning, colourful window displays and amazed at the numbers of people going through the doors. Visiting Harrods is a must for everybodys bucket list.
There were over three hundred departments in the store. It was completely overwhelming. The shop itself is arranged over several floors and takes up a whole block."I have never been in a shop like it. There is nothing to match this in Blackpool, or even

Preston.It is completely in another league."said Mum.

"Find yourself a little gift and I'll treat you" said Phil unexpectedly. The pair of them dashed to the beauty counters and Mum chose some pearlised nail varnish. "Thank you, Phil. I shall think of you when I wear this." Mum said warmly, proudly waving her Harrods bag.

We weaved our way through the oyster bar to the food halls which were bedecked with ornate colourful wall tiles, an original feature of the shop. "I absolutely love these old style wall tiles.They are so ornate."gushed Mum. She was really taken. It was wonderful to see these original touches had survived since about 1900, when the original building was replaced.

The food halls were heaving with tourists and wealthy shoppers alike, perusing over the unusual fresh salads, cakes, breads and meats of all descriptions.

Phil purchased a selection of tasty looking rolls and some sliced cold meats for our supper and these were placed carefully into one of Harrod's signature green carrier bags.

I loved the handbag department and selected a leather shiny handbag with a suede interior and a matching purse. Sadly the price tag knocked me out."Over a thousand pounds for that lovely handbag" I said" I'll come back when I have won the Lottery."

Mum's favourite was the ladies fashions, unusual, quality, expensive items."Look at these cashmere jumpers Leah" she said longingly. " They'd be just right for up North. Pity the price tag doesn't match my purse."

Wearily we took the bus all the way home after a wonderful day.It was a stop start journey but gave us the chance to rest our tired feet and shut our eyes to recoup and reflect on our day out.

Once indoors I made a welcome pot of tea and quickly laid the table. Phil laid out the rolls and cold meats. I got some pickles and salad and we all sat round enjoying the feast.

The Natural History Museum had provided amazing memories

for Mum to take back to Blackpool. It had been just her kind of thing. The Harrod's visit had opened our eyes to the wealth that exists in London.   The range and scope of items sold was incredible. The bonus of the day was that we had all got to know and understand each other better.

We had passed several homeless street people, both male and female, who would never be able to shop at Harrods. Instead they had to rely on food banks, soup kichens and handouts of bedding. They must have some stories to tell.

"They are somebody's children." Mum said sadly. "Life isn't fair." I reflected on the little baby boy that Mum had kept a secret and wondered what he would have grown up to be. "So sad" I whispered to myself with a lump in my throat. But then life is not fair.

I have been told by our neighbour George, who works at Harrods in the exclusive watch department, that Harrod's was originally founded in 1849. It is now built on a five acre patch of Knightsbridge. As the largest department store in Europe it claims to have housed the worlds first escalator.

To think that we had bought items in a shop which royalty frequents, including, in the past, beautiful Diana, Princess of Wales.

CHAPTER 12

Phil's decision

Mum went to pack her case for her train back to Blackpool and wearily I sat in the sitting room with Phil.

"Are you alright Phil" I blurted out concerned, having noticed that he was a bit down at times.

"Leah," he said. "I need to talk to you. I have been offered a job in South Africa. It is a great opportunity teaching the fundamentals of music production in Johannasberg, As you know I love African music and could listen to it all day. It is a great opportunity. I am not sure what to do."

Then he put his head in his hands in quite a desperate way. This conversation was completely out of the blue, something I hadn't expected so naturally I was very surprised

"Do you need me to help you make a decision " I said.

" Leah, I just don't know" was his reply. As ever the strong common-sense me took over.

"Come on Phil. Lets talk this through. We can make a list of the positives and negatives of this opportunity."

With that I grabbed a pen and notepad and started to make lists. Phil began to join in with his own ideas.

"I'd lose my place in this house but I'd be in the thick of the African music scene. It would be a lifetime opportunity. I have never been to South Africa. It would be a step forward in my career."

Soon we had a long list and the positives far outweighed the negatives

"Seems like I'm going to South Africa then, Leah. I had better get online and find a flight. Thanks for helping me make a decision. I have never been good at making my mind up."

"Glad I could help you" I replied.

"I'm going to book it right now, before I talk myself out of it.

For the housemates it would mean that we would have to find a new person to share or fork out extra money to cover Phil's share.

Phil came back into the room with a smile on his face. He had booked his flight and was off in one weeks time.

We talked about getting someone to cover his rent and he announced that he felt it right to give one month's rent as he hadnt given his notice soon enough. That would help us a lot and give us a bit of time to get a new person.
As I saw the other housemates I told them about Phil's decision. We had enjoyed having a man about the house. He could open the odd stubborn jar, wire the plugs, put the dustbins out and he helped us feel safe as we lived in a vulnerable area. "Hey girls" I said. "We are not a load of weak wimps. We can manage without a man in the house. Let us put an advert in and see who answers. Man or woman it doesn't matter. We can do anything!"

With Ellens help we worded the advert and placed it on Gumtree. "That's it. Done and dusted." said Ellen.

I helped Phil to pack. He didn't have a lot. Material things didn't seem important to him.

It was a sad day as we watched Phil get into his taxi to the airport, his life's belonging in one suitcase. A few hugs and kisses and we waved him off.

"We will miss you Phil." "Good Luck." "Hope it works out for you." "Keep in touch," we called as the taxi drew away. We had lumps in our throats. You don't realise how fond you can get of the people around you. After all, Phil had been like a brother to us. Someone who we could trust.

Sadly I checked his room and gave it a quick once over with the vacuum and a spray of polish. The sweet smell of the lavender polish and the spruced up room was ready to welcome a new flatmate as soon as possible. My mood slowly lifted as I came to terms with the situation. Things never stay the same.

There was always something about Phil that I couldn't put my finger on. Some mysterious thing that I couldn't fathom out. But life goes on..........

CHAPTER 13

Moving on

Phil's place in the house was quickly taken up by a friend of Ellens from Ireland, also a nurse but in Accident and Emergency. Her name was Mary and she was in her mid thirties. She was plump and jolly. Mary had lived in London before but had gone back to Ireland five years ago to help the family nurse her grandmother who lived alone, until she had died earlier this year.

Mary fitted in well. Our housemate Jessica, always the sensible one, took on the 'manager' role of the house, collecting rent and reporting anything amiss to our landlord. So now it was an all female house and all of us were unattached. It was a new era.

With a population of nearly nine million in London, an area of 607 square miles you would think that there must be just one perfect man for each of us unattached females. Only time will tell. We will keep hoping as all of us housemates had hoped to one day have a family and our biological clocks were slowly ticking away.

So the summer came and went and we carried on as usual. To cheer ourselves up Ellen and I booked for a day out in London. It was, by now, October. Luckily our shifts were compatible.
It was the first chance we have had to have a real girly catch up and we had lots to talk about. We started out by having a manicure and pedicure. Nurses spend many hours on their feet so we have learnt that it is important to treat your feet well. As we sat in the nail bar we planned the rest of our day.

"Leah, I have been thinking how we can get the most out of our day. One of the nurses told me about a great day out. Why don't we go on the Emirates Air Line, across the River Thames?" she suggested. "I have never seen it yet alone been on it. It goes

56

from near North Greenwich Underground on the Greenwich Peninsular right across the River Thames to the Royal Dock. Come on Leah. Lets go for it."

The Emirates Air Line is the cable car carrying people high over the River Thames. It is quite a new addition to the London skyline only having been built in 2012.

"Sounds like fun to me, not that I particularly like heights. I'll give it a go." I said excitedly. Before too long we were racing along with our newly revived feet and painted finger nails determined to get the most out of the day.

"Leah, don't walk so fast. I should have worn my trainers. I've only got little legs." Ellen cried. "Take bigger strides" I laughed.

I was anxious to pack as much as possible into our day so we headed to North Greenwich where the famous O2 stands. The O2 is an arena for large performances and is frequented by top stars and massive audiences. The Emirates Air Line was closeby.

We walked quickly and excitedly from the O2 to the Greenwich Peninsular and queued for our tickets for the cable car. Neither Ellen or I had never ventured on a cable car before. "Hope I can cope with this "said Ellen. "Me too. My legs are turning to jelly just looking at it" I replied. The transportation pods arrived one after another and we carefully jumped on. This piece of transport waits for no one. You have to hop on quickly. I'm not sure what would happen to you if you were not quick off the mark.

We were quickly lifted high up as the strong mechanics did their bit. There were occasional scary jerks as the pod glided over the mechanism.

In no time here we were viewing the Thames from above. "Ekkkkk" screamed Ellen. "Scary but this is awesome." I reassured her telling her that we could only fall in the River Thames below! We reached the other side and hopped off laughing. It wasn't such a bad journey after all. It took ten minutes and the unique views were spectacular. That was once we had dared to open our eyes!

We spent a while exploring this historic side of East London which was formerly dockland before finding a greasy spoon type of cafe with a kindly proprietor who served us coffee.

" Can you tell us a bit about this area." said Ellen in her soft Irish brogue.

"The Royal Albert Dock, The Royal Victoria Dock and the George V Dock were where the ships brought different cargo. It was mainly meat from Australia, New Zealand and South America." said the cafe manager. "It's all different now. A container system involving lorries and ships has replaced the manual labour and the docks are no longer used in this way." he said informatively.

"Oh, I suppose that was progress" I said.

"Yes, but it destroyed the camaraderie that this area had. Many families suffered from this change." he said with a tone of sadness in his voice, as if yearning for past times.

"I have been working here, in this cafe for fifty years. This dockland area has lost something special." he said wearily as he carried on drying up the china mugs. Ellen and I looked sadly at each other.

As we walked away we discussed what is known as 'progress'. Even in our short lives we have seen so much change and we agreed that some people adapt and some find it hard. "For better or for worse, nothing stays the same" said Ellen with a tone of sadness.

East London is a part of Lodon that is still developing. Much of the area suffered serious bombing in World War 2 and it took a long time to rebuild it.

There was a huge surge in building work going on. We could see new modern tall flats for young, successful business people which stood alongside the original council flats and nearby small houses. "I guess these houses provided homes for dock labourers and other working classes." said Ellen.

"Look Ellen" I pointed "There is the Docklands Light Railway. Phil told me all about it. "It is a driverless train which has been great for this area as it has made getting around London so much easier for people."

Quite frightening to think that a human being isn't in the driving seat, I thought. We watched and took it all in. It certainly was something special.

There, right next to the station was Excel, a smart exhibition facility, now standing at the waters edge. A far cry from the former dockside which would have thrived on blood, sweat tears and the hard grafting of the workers. In those days we would have seen barrows, bicycles, down trodden workers and scruffy boys with bare feet. How times have changed.

We inquisitively made our way over to ExCel, London, which held parking for over three thousand cars.

On the impressive approach stood a stunning sculpture called The Dockers. At three metres high, it depicted three dock workers, some in flat caps, with chains and pulleys unloading sacks of supplies. One docker was pushing an upright trolley, the type used in bygone times. It was thought provoking and struck a chord in our hearts.

I said to Ellen, "It's good that the ordinary working man is represented and remembered. " She agreed, as she took a 'photo. "Yes, those people worked so hard. It's right that they should be remembered.

Our little stop off had been a treasured delve into the past.

Back onto the Emirates Air Line for a reversal of our forward ride on the cable car. Soon we arrive safely on terra firma at the Greenwich Peninsular and after a short walk, following the signage, we came across the River bus service.

The cable car had been a great experience. "Leah" said Ellen. Wasn't I brave? I'm really proud of myself. We are having such a good time." she giggled.

CHAPTER 14

The River Bus

We didn't have to wait long for our next mode of transport which was the river bus, run by Transport for London.

We bought a ticket to the Tower of London river stop and enjoyed a coffee from the cafe facility on the river bus.

We had grabbed the front seats and so had a brilliant view as we headed towards the centre of London. The outlook was a sight to behold and the unexpected speed and power of the river bus was exciting.

We stopped at Masthouse Terrace Pier where more passengers got on.

Two young men grabbed the empty seats behind us. They were both smart, good looking, tall and seemed nice so when they started to chat to us we responded positively.

We established that they were both in the medical profession. Rishi Jain was from India and his parents who still lived in India had sent him to an English boarding school when he was 5 years old.

Michael Dixon, believe it or not, came from Preston, not far from my home town of Blackpool. Small world I thought.

At that moment I heard a voice in my head. It was my good school friend Lynne."This is your destiny, Leah Harris. Your future is mapped out already. You'll find out soon enough." I immediately dismissed these thoughts as being my silly imagination. At that point in time I had no idea of the impact that this meeting would have on my life.

We carried on our river bus journey passing very old jetties sometimes used in the film making industry and, in contrast, huge dominant tall office blocks. Our heads turned as we passed The Prospect of Whitby pub. Michael told us that this pub claims to be the oldest riverside pub dating back to 1520.

"That's what I love about London" I said. "There is so much history here." "Nowadays," Michael explained, "there are many expensive and exclusive waterside apartments that are built in the shell of warehouses. These were once used for storing tobacco." "Nearby " said Rishi "is one actually called Tobacco Dock, which is a huge warehouse dating back to the 1800's. It hosts pop up festivals and films." "I'd love to go there one day " I said.

We chatted to our new acquaintances as if we had known them for years. They were easy to talk to and there was a glimmer of an instant spark between us. They were both in their early thirties and soon they had us guessing what job they did. This gave us all a laugh as we went through everything that we could think of. Doctors, Dentists, Consultants, Nurse, Obstetrics and Gynaecology, Radiologist, Physiotherapist and a heap more suggestions. We hadn't guessed correctly until Ellen finally got it. "Pharmacists." "Yay" emphasised Rishi the dark guy ."You got it." We all laughed. "Hospital life can be fun but it is usually manic." We agreed.

The two young men had met whilst working in the Pharmacy Department of a hospital at Tooting, south London. Like us, they had the day off and had wanted to make the most of their time. The pair had come up to see a few sights in London and to spend some time in a bar that they had heard of called the Aqua Shard. This, they advised, is found high up on the thirty first floor of London's tallest building, which boast 87 floors and is part of the new glass building that dominates the skyline called The Shard. It can't be missed. It sits dwarfing the next door London Bridge station. The two young men had been told that the Aqua Shard was an experience with amazing views. Their eyes lit up when they cheekily said "Plus a bit of alcohol never goes amiss!"

Rishi and Michael invited us to join them for a drink at the Aqua Shard. Ellen and I looked at each other and we could tell that we were both keen on this idea.

To get to there we had to take a walk across the beautiful, iconicTower Bridge, standing closeby the imposing Tower of London. Once on the bridge, we stopped to admire the magnificent detail of the Tower of London. For those who don't know, the Tower is where London Beefeaters can sometimes be spotted in their unusual and immaculate uniforms. In olden times the smart Beefeaters would have been responsible for safeguarding the Crown Jewels and looking after prisoners kept at the Tower. Today the Beefeaters are the ceremonial guardians of the Tower. They attract tourists for photographs and give guided tours.

We reflected on some of the Towers history. Ellen, using her phone, Googled the Tower of London to check on her knowledge of Henry VIII's wives. She was right. Ellen confirmed that both Anne Boleyn and Catherine of Aragon had been beheaded at the Tower of London. "I remembered that from school" she laughed. "That's gruesome. Thank goodness times have changed for the better." said Rishi.

Amazingly this popular and historical tourist attraction dates right back to about 1066 and was built after the Norman Conquest.

"If you lived a long life and studied the history of London everyday, you'd never run out of things to do and learn" said Rishi. "Come on. The Aqua Shard isn't far."

I walked along with Rishi and Ellen with Michael. With our medical backgrounds we had plenty to chat about. Ellen was never short of anything to say anyway.

Heading towards the Shard we passed the shopping mall, Hay's Galleria, formerly Hay's Wharf and now a grade 2 listed building housing restaurants, flats and shops. We came to the Mayor of London's offices, City Hall, a modern strangely shaped round building. "Wow, London certainly has some stunning and unusual buildings. I hadn't quite realised " said Rishi." In the past I took London for granted. Just another place. Now I can see how beautiful London looks." I had to agree. The sun had come out and everywhere looked bright and inviting, challenging the reputation of London's weather being overcast, grey and damp. Alongside the river we saw Her Majesty's Ship Belfast, that once belonging to the Royal Navy, We used Goggle to find a bit more about it. It was now permanently moored on the Thames as a Museum ship and part of the Imperial War Museum. The ship, which dated back to 1936, had been very active in World War 2. It was finally put to reserve in 1963, along with its secrets and memories.

The Shard soon came into sight. It was shimmering in the sun like huge blades of glass, hence it's name. We had to stop, look up at it and wonder. How had it been built to such a height? The wonders of modern engineering were beyond our comprehension.

We took the lift up to the Aqua Shard bar where we were bowled over by the views. Taking a comfy seat we chatted and shared a bottle of wine. It felt quite magical and exciting to be so high up, in such pleasant company and surroundings." I feel on top of the world" gushed Ellen in her lilting Irish accent.

Michael told us that he enjoyed history and visiting historical sites, in particular historical battlegrounds. He belonged to a medieval re-enactment club that focussed on re-enacting European history in the period from the fall of Rome to about the end of the 15th Century. He was full of enthusiasm for his hobby and described his medieval outfits. Ellen looked amazed. "What fun" she said. Ellen enjoyed everything! She just loved life and people.

Rishi explained that he belonged to a London rambling club. They met twice a month, once on a varying weekday and once on the second Sunday in every month and he would drive to a starting point and park his car and do a circular walk with a pub lunch. He said that with work he couldn't always make it but he went as often as he could. He looked fit, dashing and slender, the walking having agreed with him. "It helps me to relax and enjoy the beautiful countryside. I think I was influenced having spent my boarding school days in Somerset. You must join me on a ramble one day Leah " he said.

My heart jumped. "That would be nice" I replied with a smile and a positive tone. My thoughts drifted to the walks I had enjoyed when dating Dan and my trip to Box Hill with Phil. How I too had enjoyed the challenge, the views and fresh air. "I would like that very much. I love walking and miss the countryside."

We seemed to feel very comfortable in each others company. I suppose the wine helped. Soon we were sharing our second bottle! It was like we had known each other for years. Something had clicked. Ellen's eyes were alive and sparkling too. Was it the Chardonnay or maybe it was more?

We left the Shard and made our way to a well known vegetarian restaurant for a delicious meal before heading back to our homes on the train from London Bridge station.
"I'll be in touch" Rishi said in his kind voice. My heart missed a beat. We kissed goodnight and I sensed there was something special between us. Rishi gave my nose a little pinch and squeezed my hand. I think we may have fallen for each other.
I was dazzled by the events that I had experienced on this great day, the Emirate Air line, the thrilling ride on the river bus, the ancient beauty of The Tower, the glamorous Aqua Shard bar. The very best part of everything was meeting Rishi, the tall, dark, handsome Indian who was polite, kind and generous........ and that long passionate kiss as we parted.

I hoped there would be more days like this to come.

CHAPTER 15

The Waiting Game

That night I had one of my long conversations with Mum. Naturally she liked to be kept in the loop with the details of events in my life. Since coming to London I had kept her updated with any potential boyfriends so I told her all about Rishi, the suave dark skinned Asian, our meeting on the river bus and the power I had sensed in our connection. "Mum, he really is special. Let us hope he gets in touch. I can't sleep at night thinking about him." "I have never heard you speak about any of your boyfriends like this before" said Mum.

We chuckled that both Rishi and Michael were in the medical profession like Ellen and me. What were the chances of that, all four of us working in the National Health Service? I told Mum that Rishi had suggested that I join him for a ramble one day with his club. "He is a really handsome Hindu Mum. He went to a school in England from the age of five and comes from a town near Delhi called Jaipur. It's known as the pink city. He is a pharmacist and has huge soft brown eyes. You would love him."

Mum had always been very accepting of different cultures and I had been brought up the same way. "It's one world" she would say.

We spoke about Ellen and how well she had got on with Michael. Mum had met Ellen when she came to the house. She had thought her a lovely young woman, a happy and bubbly person. I agreed. She was just right to raise your spirits and make you laugh. "Great qualities for a nurse." I said.

Mum told me that she had bumped into my ex, Dan, in town. He had asked her to send me his love. My views hadn't changed. I was just not interested at all. I said that I wished he would move on. Now I had Rishi in my life or so I thought....

A month went by and I hadn't heard from Rishi. For me it felt like a tragedy. It didn't make sense because I had experienced the magic between us, so I felt devastated. There definitely had been something there I told myself. It wasn't one sided. It's not my imagination. I know it isn't.

I had given Rishi my phone number and my email address written on the back of my hairdressers appointment card but all had gone quiet. Not a phone call or email. What had gone wrong?

All I could do was to wait as I had no way to contact Rishi except through Ellen and I wouldn't do that. I don't chase men. It is a rule of mine. I let them do the chasing. Even though I felt shaken, disappointed and let down as things hadn't worked out as I thought, I wasn't going to make the first move.
I hadn't seen Ellen as our shifts were different. You wouldn't believe that you can live in the same house as someone and work at the same hospital but not see them. I had heard however, on the grapevine, that Ellen's relationship was going well and she had been seeing a lot of Michael. I was pleased for her but it made my emptiness and longing even worse.

I went over and over the day that I had spent with Rishi. The closeness we felt and the way we chatted like we had known each other for years. What on earth had gone wrong? The not knowing made it hurt even more. Because I am a strong woman I thought I wouldn't let this get the better of me but when you feel you have met your soul mate it's not so easy to forget.

I worked so hard on the ward all that month trying to put Rishi at the back of my mind. The patients were demanding, the paperwork endless and the hours long We were short-staffed due to nurses moving on through promotion or to new jobs out of London. You couldn't blame them as some went where their wages would stretch further due to lower rent. Keeping busy was taking my mind off Rishi. In fact when working I didn't get much of a chance to even think about him, so perhaps that was a blessing. The weather had turned bitterly cold and the ward was full with patients with broken bones due to icy pavements.

Exhausted after one late shift, I couldn't wait to get back to the house for what little remained of the evening. I turned on the computer to check my emails and saw that Rishi had sent me a message.

My heart was pounding with excitement and trepidation. "I knew it, I knew it" I shouted out to myself. He hadn't forgotten me after all. Nervously I clicked on to see what it said.

Hi Leah, I have been out of the country to see my family in Jaipur, Rajasthan. It was an unexpected trip to see about important family business. I'm so sorry that I didn't get a chance to email you. I stupidly forgot to take the email address and mobile number with me. I left them in my flat and nobody could get hold of them for me. Sorry if I have caused you anguish. I'm wondering if you have a Sunday or a day off in the week that would fit in with the rambling club and if not would you like to have a day out with me?'

My heart missed a beat. This explained everything. A feeling of relief spread over me. It was going to be alright. I thought it best not to answer straight away as I was tired and I didn't want to appear too overpowering. I needed to think carefully about the wording of my reply.

The next evening, having mulled over my answer, I took the chance to reply. I told Rishi that I thought he had forgotten all about me and that I would love a day out if we could find a day when we were both off work and the rambling club were meeting. If that wouldn't work maybe we could do our own thing. A walk along the River at Kingston or a night in town along the London Canals or perhaps visit Chinatown, near Leicester Square. We were spoilt for choice.

I'd leave it to Rishi. I put my mobile number on the email just to be sure that he'd got it.

Lo and behold that evening he called me. We chatted endlessly and made an arrangement to go for a walk in Kingston the following Friday. Our shift patterns didn't coincide with his rambling club. It was probably better just the two of us anyway, especially as we were still getting to know each other and it would be our first proper date.

Friday came round quickly. I got off the train at Kingston. I felt excited yet a bit scared. I had put such a lot of hope into this relationship since getting Rishi's email and the subsequent phone call. Could our friendship develop into something more?

I spotted Rishi at our arranged meeting point and hurried towards him. Rishi put his strong arms around me and we kissed. At that moment I could tell that this was the start of something big. For a minute or two there was just us two in our own little world.

Holding hands firmly we wandered on the south side of the river, heading towards beautiful Hampton Court and passing through a 750 acre park. Deer descending from Henry VIII era were roaming free, not caring about the passing humans. It was a peaceful and natural environment.

The weather was being kind to us and although chilly the sun came out intermittently.

Rishi told me all about his visit to Jaipur, though he didn't expand on his sudden and unexpected reason for going. We spoke generally about life and work. Chatting came easily and was natural to both of us.

Eventually we got onto the subject of Jaipur, his family home. I asked him about the famous pink buildings. Story has it that in 1876, the then Prince of Wales and Queen Victoria had visited India on a tour. Pink apparently denotes the colour of hospitality. He said that it was a Maharaja who had the buildings painted pink.

Rishi then told me about some of the celebrations that Jaipur held annually. The Elephant Festival, usually held in March, where elephants are paraded bedecked with bright vibrant brocade embellishments and heavy jewellery, alongside horses, camels and colourful folkdancers. "Wow." I said."That must be a sight to be seen.I love elephants and hope I can see that for myself one day" Rishi was so interesting.

We reached Hampton Court and enjoyed a warming soup in the cafe. The days were short and dusk was approaching as we crossed the river to return home. We stopped and watched the river flowing for a while then Rishi held me in his arms and kissed me passionately. I felt the magic between us like I'd never felt with anyone before.

We held hands tightly as we made our way to the station, neither saying a word, lost in thought.

I left Rishi at Clapham Junction to make his way home and me to mine."I'll message you" he said quietly. "Great " I smiled. "Please don't leave it too long or you will break my heart." I murmured.
It had been a wonderful day.

Before I collapsed into my bed I thought it right to speak to my friend Lynne. I was excited to tell her that I was besotted by this amazing new man in my life.

"I told you " she said knowingly .....

CHAPTER 16

More than colleagues

London is a wonderful place. I have come to the conclusion that the saying 'If you're tired of London, you're tired of life' is one hundred per cent true. It is a great city and there is always something happening somewhere. It's easy to find out what's on through the Internet, newspapers and local notices.

Because nurse wages can't always stretch to expensive outings and London can be ridiculously costly my new friends and I have found cheaper alternatives by socialise locally.

The circle of hospital friends try to meet up weekly at a nearby wine bar for a bit of relaxation. The group are great fun and we all have the hospital experience in common so, as you might imagine, much of the conversation is around work, the characters and the funny incidents that occur on a regular basis.

After a couple of glasses of Pinot we are all laughing. Sometimes we share our sadness when we have lost someone on the wards or in surgery, especially if they are young. It helps to share the grief and emotion. We counsel and support each other at these times. We see many serious cases at our hospital because it is famous for its pioneering work. For over thirty years the hospital has been instrumental in early liver transplants and liver disease and that is just one of the departments. Groundbreaking work takes place all over the hospital.The newly built helipad assists seriously ill patients to get lifesaving treatment quickly following terrible car crashes and suchlike.We all have a sense of pride in being part of such a great organisation.

A group like ours helps to normalise life and keep things in perspective. We celebrate the fun things, like each others birthdays and engagements. It keeps our feet on the ground when experiencing sadness and tragedy through everyday occurences.

These friends are strong people, like brothers and sisters to me, something I have never had being an only child.

I told the group all about Rishi and how I'd fallen for him. "I can tell you are smitten." said Verna, a jolly nurse from A and E. I could feel myself blushing. "Yes, your are right Verna" I replied softly as I recalled our day out and my inner feelings.

It was after one of these gatherings that I was surprised, even shocked, that Phil had been trying to call me on my mobile. Not being able to get me he had resorted to sending me an email. It was the first time he had bothered to contact me since he went to his new music job in Johannesburg.

The message read,
'Hi Leah,
Just to let you know that I shall be returning from South Africa at the end of the month.
   I haven't enjoyed the new job. I didn't relate to my line manager very well and things kind of went downhill and pear shaped.
   I wondered if there is any space in the house for me to live back there'?
Much love, Phil.'

He signed off with a string of emojis.

The next day, snatching a free moment, I sent a message back. Here was my reply.

'Dear Phil,
  Great to hear from you and I am sorry that things didn't work out for you in Johannesburg.
I'm sure you will get on your feet again once back in London.
   Unfortunately there is no vacancy at the house right now. We have a nurse called Mary who has taken your room and every-one else is staying at the moment.

I'd like to meet up with you and I know that Jessica, Jasmine and Ellen would too. Maybe you'd like to come to the house for a meal or we could meet up somewhere once you are settled? Lots has been happening for me recently. I will have to tell you if we meet up.

Leah.'

Phil was the sort of man that was in his own world and oblivious of others. The caring nurse in me had picked up on the fact that Phil was depressed and down so I tried to be kind. Mental health is a terrible thing and I wasn't going to fuel any depression. London can feel lonely and if I didn't have my hospital wine bar group and the housemates I too would be lonely.

Phil had neither of these friendships in his life at present, so I reached out a helping hand to him.

Two weeks later I found myself sitting in a popular local Chinese restaurant with Phil. Jess and Ellen came along too to give support.

Things had looked up. I was glad to hear that Phil had managed to find a place in a shared flat with someone from Sussex, a mate from his former school.

I told Phil about Rishi and that our relationship was going well. He seemed pleased for me.

We chatted about old times and teased him about the fact that he never took his turn to wash up. It was all light hearted as we reminisced about his time at the hose.

Phil had some interviews lined up with a strong possibility of work. He had made a lot of contacts in the world of music so hopefully things will work out for him.

We agreed to stay in touch. I noticed that Phil had perked up and appeared to be more upbeat, hopefully conquering his touch of depression.

Let's hope he gets work and bounces back to his old self.

CHAPTER 17

A Visit to the Hindu Temple

The months flew by and soon winter and spring had passed and we began to experience the warmer days and longer evenings.

Rishi and I had continued to be a couple and our love for each other was evident. It was a great feeling. We were making memories together and developing a stronger relationship as the months whizzed by.

In early June Rishi took me to BAPS Shri Swaminarayan Hindu Temple in Neasden, London. Indira, a lovely nurse at work had told me all about the temple after I had told her about Rishi being a Hindu.

"You just have to go there" she said. "It is beautiful. Words can't do it justice. It's marble and a most unusual sight in London. You will learn a lot about Hinduism too"

So, I asked Rishi to take me there. "That's fine by me. I didn't think that you were interested in Hinduism, but I'm so pleased that you are" he said.

We travelled on train, bus and underground right across London on a quest to see the Hindu Temple for ourselves.

We turned a suburban corner and the temple came in sight. "Oh Rishi" I said "Look. It is amazing. "

The sun was shining on this huge white marble building which stood out against the blue sky. "It is designed to bring together Gods and humans" said Rishi. "It is a sanctuary for Hindu worshippers."

Rishi had done some research before our visit and he had learnt all about the temple's origin. He so wanted me to get a lot out of the visit, bless him. Apparently it was built by traditional methods and a lot of the preparation building work was carried out in India by skilled craftsmen. One thousand volunteers had helped to assemble it when, once completed, the prepared pieces were shipped over to London. Work began in 1992 and by 1993 it was ready for worship as an important sanctuary for Hindu worshippers.

"Come on Leah, lets go inside." said Rishi tugging at my arm. I want you to see everything." Respectfully we entered and immediately removed our shoes. Rishi explained that symbolically removing shoes represents leaving behind all earthly and wordly activities. We were directed to the Mandir, the place of worship. We came across a stunning marble temple where we could see several shrines. Volunteers from the Hindu religion were keeping a watchful eye on the streams of visitors. London school children, on their best behaviour, were on a day trip as part of their National Curriculum. "Isn't that great Rishi. School-children learning about different religions by an educational visit."I whispered. "It is so important" agreed Rishi.

Despite the large numbers of people visiting the temple was peaceful and harmonious. The atmosphere was calming and uplifting

We wandered about absorbed in this new experience. I was mesmerised by the sanctum which was the focal point. There was an amazing round domed ceiling which I just couldn't take my eyes off. How beautiful. "Wonderful workmanship, such skill." I whispered.

We silently spent time at each shrine where figures of deities were placed behind glass. They were offered water, fruit, flowers and incense daily. Many intricate and beautifully carved marble columns formed part of the building and depicted different deities. We were hand in hand, wondering at this spectacle, a testament to Hindu architecture.

As we left the Mandir Rishi told me that strict followers do not eat meat, drink any alcohol, steal, have sex before marriage and always follow a pure lifestyle.

"The majority of Hindus have a shrine in their homes. It can be a room, a small altar, pictures or a statue" explained Rishi. There was so much to learn about this religion and I was completely bowled over.

Once out of the Mandir we had the opportunity to ask a volunteer guide some questions about the fabulous carvings. He told us that carving had been undertaken by 650 artisans in India. The building had been made from 2000 tons of white marble and at a cost of 12 million pounds, much of which was raised by followers of the faith.

Just before reclaiming our shoes we visited the gift shop and I purchased some lavender incense sticks and half a dozen colourful bangles as a souvenir of this amazing visit.

For me it had been an unusual place to have been but I was so pleased that I had experienced this priviledge. The fact that I came with Rishi, a Hindu himself, had made it even more special. This visit had bonded our love and understanding making us stronger as a couple. So our love grew.

CHAPTER 18

Summetime

Rishi and I spent more and more time together. With the light evenings we made the most of our free time from work. We packed in lots of days out and made wonderful memories together.

We joined the local gym, went on long walks, away day trips to the coast and visited the London art galleries. We enjoyed several visits to the Kensigton Museums, National Trust Properties and Royal Parks.

Rishi was full of stories about his life at boarding school, his parents in Jaipur and his work as a Pharmacist. I could listen to him endlessly as he had a very beguiling style.

We had become a couple with all that it means. I found that I was deeply in love with Rishi. I couldn't have imagined my life without him.

We popped up to Blackpool to stay a couple of nights to see my Mum. It was their first face to face meeting, although they had chatted several times on Facetime and on the mobile. She thought Rishi to be polite, charming and very good looking. We had hoped to see my schoolfriend Lynne but she was in Turkey with her mother who was brushing up on her belly dancing skills.

Our first day was spent on the sandy beach where we paddled, relaxed and sunbathed. The weather was beautiful. Blue cloudless skies and lots of sunshine and a warm balmy breeze. It was the kind of perfect day that you never forget. In the evening we went to see the wonderful singer, Alfie Boe, performing in the Blackpool Winter Garden. This was an amazing and beautiful building dating back to the 1870's. It had lots of retro charm, something Rishi and I both loved. There was a ballroom, a bar, a theatre and business complex with decor from a bygone era, tiles, marble and palm trees.

After the show we headed to a table in the bar and Rishi went to buy drinks. His phone was on the table. There was a whistle from a newly arrived text message.

I shouldn't have looked at the message but something inside me told me to.

Feeling guilty I quickly looked to see who had sent the message. On Rishi's screen I read the word 'Mum.'

I clicked onto the mesage. 'Call me Rishi. Serious problem with Annika' it said.

Rishi returned to the table and looked at his message. He looked very worried and stared ahead blankly deep in thought. He didn't say anything and I didn't ask. He was distant for the rest of the evening.

In the morning Rishi took himself to the bottom of the garden at Mum's house. From the kitchen window I watched him, though he didn't know I was there.
He made a call. What was said I will never know but it was obviously something quite serious and Rishi came back indoors and seemed upset.
Rishi was no longer his usual attentive self. He was very quiet, withdrawn and secretive. Something was amiss. I asked him if he was alright. Was there anything worrying him? He didn't answer, but just took my hand. squeezed it and looked longingly into my eyes. Eventually he whispered the words "Trust me".

We went back to London but things were not quite right. The phone call had cast a dark cloud on our trip up North. I had no idea about Rishi's call and the change in his behaviour. From being gloriously happy I was now seriously worried and the fact that he was keeping whatever had happened to himself. He had always been so open with me, sharing his worries but now I felt like he was covering something up. Who was this person Anneka and what was the serios problem that I read about on Rishi's 'phone?

This, I thought could be the start of the biggest heartbreak that I have ever encountered and I couldn't bear it.

That evening I sent Lynne an email hoping she was enjoying the belly dancing holiday and telling her that we were sorry that we hadn't been able to meet up. I felt that I needed re-assurance from Lynne after the phone message that Rishi had received and his sudden change in character.
Lynne replied almost immediately telling me that there was no point in worrying. 'Worry does nothing' she wrote. ' It will work out one way or another. Your future with Rishi is already decided. Just accept the situation which may be testing for you. Life doesnt always run smoothly.'

Lynne had such belief in destiny but her message did nothing to solve my concerns.

Once I had got back into the demanding swing of work I was obliged to put my worries behind me. It was only a chance conversation with Jessica from the house that I began to get suspicious. Jessica and I spent one evening in our tiny garden with a bottle of wine enjoying the balmy summer evening and a girly chat. Jessica told me of someone she had befriended at work who was unhappy. Her family in India had chosen a husband for her."The wedding had been arranged and poor girl hadn't even met the groom." Jessica said. We discussed the pros and cons of arranged marriages when suddenly an awful thought came into my mind. "Oh no! Could this be Rishi's problem? Maybe his family were arranging a marriage for him to someone that he didn't know."
Rishi had told me that his family were very traditional and quite strict. They followed their culture without exemption.

"Surely not an arranged marriage for my Rishi?" I murmured. My imagination was going wild. He is mine and I'm not letting anything get between us. If this suspicion is true I shall fight with everything I have. Could this explain Rishi's mobile message from his mother when we were in Blackpool? Could this account for Rishi's strange behaviour? The distant and secretive way Rishi behaved and why he was upset and couldn't tell me what was wrong. I needed to get to the bottom of this.

CHAPTER 19

Confronting suspicion

I decided to challenge Rishi about the way he had behaved in Blackpool plus his distant manner when we got back to London.

I had to wait until I had the right moment. In the meantime I Googled some research on arranged marriages so I had my facts straight.

Rishi 's family were of the Hindu religion. Arranged marriages were common in his family's part of India. A lot of arranged marriages were to preserve the heritage and culture of the Hindu religion.

Apparently parents and relatives choose a life partner for their children considering the caste where similar castes are matched. Educational backgrounds and professional status of the couple in question are compared and closely partnered for both sons and daughters. The marriage is expected to survive on commitment and duty which is considered to be a strong base.

What we had which was a real love for each other. I made a commitment to myself. I was not going to give Rishi up without a fight. Rishi knew nothing of my suspicions and I could be wrong.........

As soon as the right moment came I decided that I would challenge Rishi. Of course I could be totally wrong but what else could it be about?

Rishi and I decided to go to Folkestone for a walk on the North Downs. I saw this day as my opportunity to speak to him about my fears.

The day out was on the new HS1 high speed train from St Pancras Station,London. The station was an experience in itself with shops selling vibrant quality goods to both visitors and business people alike. Some were waiting for the Eurostar to the continent, so were chooosing souvenirs. Others purchasing last minute special gifts for wives and families or a snack for their journey. It was vibrant and buzzing.

Rishi was quite interested in trains and as I have mentioned, we both enjoyed walking. This day out together combined lots of our interests.

I hoped that the right moment would give me the chance to bring up the uncertainties surrounding the possible arranged marriage. Maybe my imagination had gone wild and I had things completely out of proportion.

Our train journey was unbelievably fast and in 55 minutes we were in Folkestone, a coastal town which had been an important sea port.

Folkestone stands on the south eastern edge of the North Downs in Kent. Rishi had downloaded a walk from the Internet and soon we found the well marked footpath of the North Downs Way.

We ascended the downs and walked steadily for an hour before stopping for a lunch. We chatted about work and our friends, Michael and Ellen who were still together.

I had prepared some home made lemonade and filled some crusty rolls. I had hastily bought some vegetable samosas knowing that these were a favourite of Rishis and together with fruit we had a plentiful healthy lunch, quite a treat.

We found a lovely viewpoint to sit. It looked over the English Channel. Again, a perfect day with clouds like balls of cotton wool set against a bright blue sky and a clam, blue sea. We always seemed to be lucky on our special days out.

Once we had eaten I asked Rishi to tell me about why he had gone quiet and into himself when we were visiting Mum in Blackpool and why something seemed to still be bothering him. I told that I wanted the absolute truth.

What he said next wasn't a complete surprise, though it wasn't what I needed or wanted to hear.

"Leah," he said in a concerned tone of voice, "my parents have arranged for me to get married to a woman who I have met only once. Her name is Annika and she is from Jaipur.

You will remember that I went to Jaipur soon after we first met. Well, that was to meet Annika, my parents choice for me. I didn't want to go but was obliged to.
The 'phone text message was to say that her mother had been rushed into hospital. Fortunately, she is now recovering well.

The main problem is my parents are expecting the arranged marriage to go ahead. It is accepted as a matter of honour by my family."

I felt a huge surge inside me. It was still a shock ,although partly expected. For a while I was speechless and my hands were shaking. I took a deep breath and got my thoughts together. My mind was whirling round in a frenzy.

The mother of my first love, Dan, had got in the way of our love. This had forced me to make a lifechanging decision. I had left my hometown and moved to London. Now Rishi's parents are doing the same by arranging a marriage to a girl that he has met only once and doesn't love.

In this day and age why can't these people stand up to their parents, I thought. I do understand that this is a slightly different situation to that of Dan as it is a cultural issue for Rishi. I feel that he is trapped by loyalty to his family and their values.

For a while we sat silently. We didn't speak. We were lost in thought. Eventually I put my arms around Rishi and told him how much I loved him and that he needed to make a choice between an arranged marriage or me. I had made my decision although this could break my heart forever.

I will never know where I got the strength to give Rishi the options. It put my love for Rishi and our futures together at risk of rejection.

We continued our walk deep in thought. The situation had spoiled the earlier happy atmosphere. We were both old enough and mature enough to know that we had something special between ourselves and that we had to deal with this situation soon, make decisions and come to conclusions.

We caught a train back to London. Our mood was low as we had a lot to think about. The normal natural chatter between us had gone as we thought deeply about our futures, whether they be together or apart.

Folkestone will always be a place that I will never forget because it was where Rishi and I faced up to lifechanging decisions that need to be finalised.

At St Pancras we went our separate ways, but before we did we kissed passionately. I had a little cry on Rishi's shoulder. Kind, as he always was, Rishi comforted me and I could see his huge brown warm eyes fill with tears. We had so much to lose. "Give me time" he said

CHAPTER 20

Waiting ....

Over a week went by and Rishi and I hadn't communicated purposely even once. We had agreed that we needed time to think things over yet not hearing was stressful. I found it hard to concentrate and walked about in a bit of a dream feeling like the world was on my shoulders. It wasn't the best time of my life and I hated being left in the lurch not knowing my future.

I turned to my computer and relentlessly played the last scene of Swan Lake with the dramatic Tchaikovsky music pulling a deep and passionate love one way and then another. It brought tears to my eyes, yet repeatedly I had to listen.

Eventually my phone rang and it was Rishi's kind voice. "Hi Leah" he said "Can we meet? I have had some time to think and want to discuss my thoughts with you"

We arranged to meet in Kingston, one of our favourite places, the following Friday. It couldn't come quickly enough. An early autumn had arrived so a walk along the River Thames to Surbiton, a bit of lunch and time to discuss the situation was our plan.

The day arrived and we met. Rishi seemed pleased to see me. I held back a bit as I didn't know what was in his head. In the back of my mind I wondered what Rishi had decided..... me or an arranged marriage.

There was much needed new legislation relating to forced arranged marriages in England, but this protects vulnerable young girls from being forced to marry someone that they do not want to.

There is a big difference between an arranged marriage and a forced marriage. As an adult male Rishi's situation was quite different, though some of the strong values like family dishonour and broken promises need to be understood and considered.

The walk was beautiful and the day was temperate and tranquil. We took in all the scenery, passing moorings of cosy houseboats along the River Thames.

Swans were abundant,appearing to swim along effortlessly without a care. Occasionally dipping their long necks into the water searching for food.

I told Rishi that I felt just like a swan gliding effortlessly while I was in absolute turmoil beneath the surface, like a swan furiously paddling to keep going. Rishi gave me a hug. " We can talk about the situation later, over lunch, so stop worrying." he said. That sounded positive I thought.

The trees were beginning to change colour. Some were a beautiful golden colour and occasional leaves dropped to the towpath in the gentle breeze. The footpath was a popular walking route linking Kingston upon Thames with Surbiton and many members of the public were making the most of the warm autumnal sunshine.
We reached Surbiton, a delightful part of the Borough of Kingston upon Thames. It held a mixture of Art Deco houses, 19th century town houses and small courtyards and had a bustling high street.

Rishi took me to a little French restaurant for lunch. It was delightful. A table for two tucked privately in a quiet corner was perfect. This is the time that my future is to be decided I thought and my hands began to shake with the thought of what was coming.

We chose from a menu and Rishi ordered some wine. I looked at the menu and thought I'd choose something small to eat as my stomach was churning with anticipation, fear and the unknown.

Rishi tasted and approved the wine and the waiter poured out two glasses. We sat back and waited for our food to arrive. Rishi didn't seem to want to make eye contact with me. I could see he was thinking of the best way to deliver his news.

I jumped in." Rishi, I need to know. I can't wait to hear what you are going to tell me a minute longer. I have waited too long already." He looked a bit surprised at the way I had reacted. I was impatient for his news.

Rishi took my hand and held it tightly. "Leah, I have made a big decision. I am going to Jaipur to discuss our serious situation with my parents. As you know they are strict Hindu's, very set in their ways, with strong views and family values. If they have made promises they would want to and expect to honour them. I am going to tell them all about you and that we love each other deeply. I will tell them that our love is true love not something that we hope will develop as in an arranged marriage.

 I shall tell them both that I cannot possibly marry Anneka. It is ridiculous to expect me to agree to an arranged marriage. I have absolutely no feelings for her.

I was sent to an English boarding school at the age of five and have spent more time in England than my country of birth. How can my parents anticipate that I can suddenly switch to a Hindu way of life. I feel pressurprised. I am really unhappy about all this and the effect it is having on me. I can't sleep at night with all the worry.

Obviously I can't predict their reaction and the outcome at this stage but I want you to know that I have fallen deeply in love with you and I will always love you whatever the outcome of my discussions with my family. It may be that my family will want nothing more to do with me"

Once again I was being left in the lurch not knowing my future. Once again I had met a man who was ruled by his mother. This time it was worse. As an Englishwoman I was unfamiliar with arranged marriages and felt lost and out of control. The man that I had fallen for had a family with different values and traditions and this was coming between us because of his parents.

I ate my lunch in silence. Rishi too. The situation didn't warrant words. We walked hand in hand to Surbiton Station for the trains home and could only stare sadly at each other. In all my life I had never experienced such a devastating blow. At a time when we should be happy with our love for each other we had this enormous problem hanging heavily over our future.

We kissed goodbye before we went our separate ways but the normal passion had been overtaken by the situation.

I walked away not knowing whether or not I'd ever see Rishi again. I felt devastated.

The next couple of months are a haze. Rishi and I met up but with our futures undecided and the pressures of work it was not a happy time for either of us. However, when we did see each other the love that we shared was evident. Rishi tried to get flights back to India to speak to his parents but due to the Christmas rush everything was booked up. In all my life I had never experienced such frustration.

CHAPTER 21

New Years Eve and Jessica is 30!

Christmas came and went. Mary and I both worked through. Surprisingly, I heard from Ellen that Rishi had flown to Jaipur to see his parents. He had, at last, managed to get a flight.

Michael had told Ellen to break it to me gently as he knew I was in a bit of an emotional state and would be exhausted after my long Christmas shifts.

At least the situation of not knowing whether my relationship was on or off was going to be finalised one way or another. Thank goodness that I won't have to wait much longer for an answer.

Rishi is at least doing something about it by going to his parents, not just letting the situation fester, I thought.

Jessica's birthday falls on New Years Eve and her big 30 was looming. After all the comings and goings over the Christmas period and now with all housemates safely back from far and wide it seemed to Jessica a great opportunity to combine her big birthday with a New Year party at the house.
"Can you and Mary help me to organise it Leah? "asked Jessica. Jess was such a lovely bubbly person.Who could say no to Jessica? Always kind and caring. So together we made a list of people to invite and the drinks and food that would be needed.

The guest list included all of the housemates, Jessica's long-standing boyfriend David together with Ellen and Michael, the pharmacist she had been dating for a while. You will recall that they had met on the Thames river bus when I met Rishi.

Jasmine was back in the country so she was invited with her

latest partner Si. We added a few friends from work and a couple of larger than life characters who could sometimes be irritating personalities but ideal in a party environment. They were good at socialising and joke telling!

Jess said she'd like to invite Phil, our former housemate who still worked the music industry; our house manager who went to South Africa. I reminded myself that when we had all met up he was simply just a friend, even though there was one point in my life when I wanted more. Anyway, a lot of water had gone under the bridge since Phil had left the house. Jessica had a good idea by suggesting that we ask Phil to take responsibility for the party music, being that he worked in the industry. "He will be great at getting the party started " I said.

We decided to keep the food simple. Mary had a good reputation for making a tasty chicken curry and rice." Most people like a good curry" she said when we asked her. We would include some vodka jellies to get the party going!
We wanted to make the house look welcoming with some birthday balloons, silly hats and a few New Year banners and accessories. Jess got the invitations out and most people could make it. Phil agreed to come and take responsibility for the music.He said that he was really pleased to get invited as he thought everyone had forgotten him. He promised to bring a glitter ball and some coloured spotlights to add atmosphere. He said he'd put a collection of songs together. He knew what got people dancing and we knew that he'd make a good job of it.

The great day arrived. It had been fun getting the party together. We had a ceiling net filled with balloons for the midnight hour. Mary was a whizz at blowing up the balloons, filling the ceiling net. We rolled the carpet back to make a better dance floor.We invited the neighbours to join us and made sure that we had enough booze for an army. We could do no more. We had thought of everything to make this dual celebration a success.

Feeling exhausted after all the preparation a quick shower

and fresh make up helped us all to perk up. We got our glad rags on and sat on our cosy settee, each with a big glass of wine. "We did it! " said Jessica. "Thanks Mary. Thanks Leah. Couldnt have done it without you. It's up to everyone else now."
We shouldn't have worried. The guests arrived and were all in the mood to party. Soon the ground floor of our rented shared home was rocking. The wine flowed, the curry was a hit, the vodka jellies were gone in minutes and Phil's expertise in his musical selection drew dancers to the floor. After a few drinks it didn't matter whether you could dance or not!

I noticed Ellen was getting on particularly well with Phil. That wasn't supposed to happen I thought. What about her Michael? He was drinking and chatting and didn't appear to have noticed Ellen giving her attention elsewhere.

As it was her birthday party Jessica had wrapped a pass-the-parcel with a selection of fun prizes. The game went down well with everyone joining into the spirit. Hoots of laughter filled the room when Phil won the top prize, a haggis! After all not only was it Jessica's birthday but it was Hogmanay and appropriate to celebrate by adding a taste of Scotland!

Of course there was the Superwoman birthday cake. Superwoman, a fictional character from the popular DC comic had been wonderfully created in the form of a sponge cake with a big candle at the side. Jessica was a true superwoman in real life and well deserving of the party.

Round about 10.30 pm we lit the birthday candle, sang Happy Birthday to Jessica and shared the cake.The fun, jokes, dancing and laughter resumed until just before midnight when the TV was turned on to full blast and the countdown to midnight began. Our ears were ringing with the noise of drunken shouting and laughter. 10, 9,8, 7, 6, ... right down to 12.00 midnight.

A huge cheer went up with shouts of Happy New Year. Big kisses, cuddles and hugs were in plenty supply.

Not wishing to miss a thing, we excitedly gathered round the TV to watch the amazing London firework display from the River Thames. Ellen then came up with a complete surprise. "Outside everyone " she ordered, "we have our own fireworks."

We duly obliged, hanging onto each other for both warmth and steadiness. The fireworks were amazing. There were lots of Oohs and Ahhs as the continuous display rose up into the sky celebrating the beginning of our new year. The alcohol had got to everyone. We joined hands with each other, trying our best at singing a couple of rounds of Auld Lang Syne. It had been a brilliant party...... except that Rishi wasn't there and I missed him so much.

CHAPTER 22

Rishi returns

Rishi was due back in a few days time. I knew that he would have the decency to get in touch with me, to tell me the outcome of the meeting with his parents.

My heart was aching as I was missing him so much and with no knowledge of the outcome of his trip I felt up in the air.

I expected to hear from him fairly soon, once he had got over his jet lag. I wasn't going to ring him, as I thought that under the circumstances he should make the first contact. Sure enough next day on a very early, dark, cold and icy morning I woke up to the ping of my phone. There was a text message from Rishi. I jumped out of bed and shakily opened up the message.

'Hi Leah. I am back. Lots to tell you. When can we meet? Rishi X'

That was it. Just a short message but a good sign was the X at the end of the message I thought.

I decided to text him back immediately as I really wanted to talk to him face to face, not discuss the situation on the' phone. I had to be off to work anyway.

My text read
' Hi Rishi. I am on earlies at the hospital today. Can we meet to-night? I'm working 7.00 am till 3.00 and off all day tomorrow, so could meet at 7pm tonight. Suggest Italian restaurant, our usual in Streatham. See you in there. Plz confirm. X Leah'

I headed off to work thinking that I needed to calm down as I had to get through this shift. Then I would go home, have an hour or so to sleep and then get myself dolled up for either the next stage of a romance or the grand finale, whatever fate had decided.

We met in the Italian as planned. Rishi was already there when I arrived and as soon as our eyes met I knew that the special thing we had between us was still there.

Rishi had bought me a single rose and laid it on the table. He looked really nice. It was obvious that he had seen the sun as he was a shade darker and was glowing with health. He looked so fit in his white shirt and tie and casual trousers. Just gorgeous. I melted.

"Wow Leah. You look stunning" he said. I had made a special effort, even wearing a flattering new dress and my high black boots. "And so do you Rishi" I said as I found my seat.

We spent the next minutes with our hands above the table, just sqeezing and holding each other's hands, looking into each others eyes, speechless, unable to utter a word.

Eventually he spoke." Leah, I have missed you so much" he said. "Me too Rishi" I whispered."Tell me all about your trip. I can't wait to hear what has happened."

"I will tell you, Leah. I will tell you exactly as it happened" said Rishi with a tone of seriousness.

Rishi went on to say that he arrived at his parents flat in Jaipur.They hadn't known that he was coming and the house-keeper told him that his parents had gone to their hill station for a change of scenery.

His parents were surprised and delighted that he had come over but seemed a bit suspicious of his motives.

His mother always fussed over him and her first thought was that he was ill or something terrible had happened. Rishi was her first born. He had a brother, Archan. She had a real soft spot and motherly love for both of her sons, as mothers usually do.

Thrilled at the thought of seeing Rishi, his parents had dashed back from the hill station to their Jaipur flat to see him and hear all about his career and life in England

They greeted each other warmly and then Rishi relayed the

event to me.

He had decided not to hold anything back but to tell his situation honestly. "Mother, Father, I respect you and all that you have done for me but I want you to know that I have fallen in love with an English lady. Her name is Leah and she is a nurse. She comes from Lancashire in the north of England but works in a London hospital. Of all the young ladies and past girlfriends that I have ever known Leah stands out. She is kind, caring, honest and shows great commitment to her work and her widowed mother. I want to marry her. I know that you have a marriage arranged for me with Anneka but I cannot marry Anneka whatever the circumstances. I love Leah with all my heart. I do not want to upset you or offend you. Please give me your blessing."

Rishi said his mother and father were in utter shock. Moments passed as this news sunk in then they eventually opened up. "How could Rishi speak like this." "Where is your loyalty and respect for your parents and family?" "What would people say?" "As a family we will never be trusted again."

His father had apparently become very angry at that point and a heated argument had followed. "Rishi, we will be the laughing stock of this city" he said. Rishi had pointed out that he had spent more of his life in England than India and how could his parents expect him to have the same strong values as they had and in any case it was his life and he was in love.

His father had argued strongly that family was everything and both loyalty and promises had to be kept. He said that he, Rishi's father, had been a great friend of Anneka's father. Her hand in marriage had been agreed by the two fathers on the deathbed of Annekas father more than twenty years ago. The marriage was arranged. Like it or not. It could not be changed. Promises could not be broken. Word is word.

His mother had to sit down, feeling faint and overcome with the unexpected visit and the heated argument. She kept shaking her head in disbelief. She had been so looking forward to

Rishi coming home for the marriage to Anneka and how could he be so cruel? Anneka would be heartbroken. How could Rishi upset his mother like this? This was the worst thing that could ever happen. How could he shatter Anneka's dreams of marriage to her eldest and dearest son? What more could he want than Anneka, such a loyal beautiful lady? Such a kind nature. And so on.....

Rishi said she went on and on so much that he told his parents that he wasn't going to argue anymore. He had made his case and it was his life. He was a grown man and could make his own decisions. He told me that he had stormed out of the family home before the argument and bad feeling got any worse. "But surely my happiness is important to you?" he had pleaded helplessly.

He then went back to his hotel and mulled over the event.

For a moment, I was speechless. I'd never heard Rishi speak with such passion.

At last, a boyfriend who is a real man, who stands up for himself. Not only do I love him for his good looks, fine and hunky figure, funny soft nature and even temperament, but I love him because he listens to and follows his heart.
Rishi continued with his story. The following day he had contacted Anneka and arranged to meet for tea at the Jai Club. Apparently Anneka had arrived early and was sitting alone at a table. Anneka had kissed Rishi on the cheek as a friendly gesture. She had a warm smile but nevertheless looked very worried. She was surprised that Rishi had come to Jaipur without even telling his family.

The important discussion had then began. Previously Rishi had, in his mind, gone over what he was going to say. How he would put the whole saga to Anneka. He had decided to be upfront and perfectly honest so without hesitation he told her the situation. He was, on no account going through with an arranged marriage as he had met and loved a young woman called Leah. He hoped she would understand.

Anneka responded very quietly."Rishi," she had said, putting her hand on his. "I am so relieved that you don't want to go through with this marriage because I too have deep feelings for somebody else.

Rishi told me that at this point he was completely taken aback.

Anneka continued, "I have had to keep my feelings for this man a closely guarded secret, for fear of upsetting your family. My mother does not even know about what I am going to tell you. It has worried me for almost a year. I have been desperate with terrible anxiety, not knowing how to get out of this situation. I have lost countless hours of sleep, tossing and turning with no idea how to solve this problem.

She went on,"We both understand the promises that were made by our parents on our behalf but we have strong, deep loving feelings for someone else that we cannot change. I only want to marry the man that I love.

Anneka then had said, " I believe that my father would want me to follow my heart, especially as I wouldn't be letting you down, Rishi. I was always his special little girl who could do no wrong. If I wanted something, I would get it. Nowdays I am still the same. i want my own way and that includes marrying the love of my life. As time has gone by, things have changed and promises made with the best intentions when a child have become irrelavant. I too have the right to refuse an arranged marriage and that is just what I will do."

Rishi looked at me. "Leah, when Anneka told me that she had fallen in love I couldn't believe what I was hearing. It was music to my ears. I can't tell you the relief that I felt. A weight had been lifted off my shoulders. It was such a release."

Anneka and Rishi had agreed that the best way forward would

be for Anneka to visit his parents to explain her side of things in a month or so, once things had calmed down and his parents had time to think things over.

"I think my parents might come round now." Rishi said hopefully.
Trying to patch things up, Rishi had gone back to see his family but both his parents had turned their backs on him and refused to speak. They would have nothing to do with him. He had calmy tried to coax them into a discussion but they were adamant that Rishi had let them down.They were unwilling to listen yet alone speak. He left them on bad terms and spent the next few days relaxing in the hotel spa whilst waiting for the days to pass until the time arrived for his flight home. He tried to bring his flight forward but it was such a busy time of year for travellers that there was no opportunity to change his ticket.

Rishi explained that those lonely days at the hotel had given him time to review his decisions and he knew that he was doing what was right for him. He would ask Leah to marry him. He was so in love and would marry Leah whatever his family thought, even if it meant cutting ties with his parents. He would stick by his decision.

In a final attempt for a peaceful solution Rishi had gone round to his parents hours just hours before his flight home. This time they wouldn't even come to the door. The housekeeper had told him that they were both 'otherwise engaged.' Rishi didn't even get the chance tell them that Anneka didn't want an arranged marriage either.

Time is a great healer so Rishi hoped that maybe they would come to terms with the situation. "We will just have to wait and see what happens next. Maybe my parents will accept the situation when Anneka has been to see them and explained her side of the story. That will throw a different light on things."

Hearing the event unfold I felt overjoyed. I jumped out of my chair and flung my arms round Rishi. "We can work things out." I said confidently." Your family wil not want to lose you." We hugged and kissed, making up for the past lost weeks.

What happened next was a complete shock. Out of the blue Rishi got down on one knee and proposed. "Please marry me, Leah." He fumbled in his pocket and shakily produced a small ring box containing a white gold engagement ring. "Yes, yes, yes. of course. " I cried excitedly.

The solitaire diamond ring was perfect, just what I had always dreamed of. Rishi slipped the ring on my finger.

The waiter, who could sense something special was happening, produced two glasses of sparkling wine on the house.

We raised out glasses and Rishi proposed a toast. "To our future together." "Yes, together forever" I replied, as tears of happiness filled my eyes. A real old fashioned proposal but right from being a little girl it was just as I had always imagined.

Once back at home, although it was rather late I rang Mum to tell her what had happened. "It's a pity that Rishi's parents can't give you their blessing, but Leah, I have never ever heard you so excited. Take a WhatsApp. photo of your engagement ring so I can show my friends on Friday! I am meeting up for lunch with Amber and Alison."

With that thought in my head I fell into my cosy bed and went into a deep sleep. The stress had been lifted. I now knew where my life was going.

CHAPTER 23

Ellen pours her heart out

Rishi sent me a message to say that Anneka had contacted him. She was leaving Jaipur to go to Australia for two months to help care for a relative in her eighties who had badly broken her leg in a fall. The Aunt was Anneka's mothers sister and she was a single lady with no family. This had been an emergency arrangement and Anneka had apologised for not been able to see Rishi's family to give her side of the arranged marriage saga.

"These things happen. I'm not letting any of it bother me. Life goes on and we are alright" said Rishi in his no nonsense style.

A week or so later Ellen knocked on my bedroom door. "Leah, can I talk to you in confidence?" Naturally I let her into the room and she took a chair and made herself comfortable. I could see that she was upset.Then for the next half hour she poured her heart out to me. Her relationship with Michael was going wrong and she had her own theories. Ellen suspected that Michael was two timing her with someone that he had connected with on an Internet dating agency. "Why would Michael go to a dating site if he already has me as his girlfriend?" she sobbed, barely able to talk through her tears.

Ellen had looked over Michaels shoulder when he was quietly on his laptop and said that she saw the evidence with her own eyes. Michael was oblivious as he was so deeply engrossed with the screen.

Now it was my turn to use my experience of getting life and relationships in perspective. Just as I had helped Phil to make a decision I used the same technique with Ellen.

"Let's make a list" I suggested. "A list of all the good things about Michael and all the things that you are not so happy about. Then we can get this relationship in perspective."

That's not going to help" she sobbed. I grabbed a pen and note-book and took no notice of Ellen's dismissive comment.

"Do you love him?" "Not sure" she said. "Is he reliable? I asked "Not really" she sobbed. "He never keeps me in the loop."

" Do you think he is mature enough for a long term relation-ship?" I asked. "Definitely not" Ellen replied. "He is actually quite immature."

I noted down her responses. We carried on in this vein. Is he hardworking? Does he have good career prospects? Does he keep his word? Does he make you laugh and is he your soulmate? Would you choose him to be the father of your children? And so on.......

Ellen gave me her honest answers. By this time she had stopped sobbing as she concentrated and thought through her answers. "OK " I said " Time for a large glass of pinot and we can review how Michael scored."

We got some wine from the fridge in the kitchen and brought it back to my room where we had a bit of a discussion about men being late developers and more immature than women and about what Ellen wanted deep down from any relationship. She confessed that she was tired of dating the wrong sorts. She had already gone through one heartbreaking experience in Ireland and felt it was time to settle down with a home and have a fam-ily before her she was too old to conceive.

"Well" I said. "Michael hasnt scored too well. He is unreliable, untrustworthy when it comes to other women, not your soul-mate and you wouldn't want him to father your children. More importantly you are not sure if you love him."

"What shall I do Leah?" she asked with a hopeless expression. "It's your decision and not for me to make your mind up. You need to own your own future." I advised. "You are a strong woman and have to make up your own mind."

"Yes, Leah. You are right. Time I got a bit tougher and had things in perspective."

I gave her a hug. "It's easier to see what others should do than sorting out your own life" I said.

Thanks Leah for your time tonight and for helping me to sort my head out. I'll sleep on it." she said taking the notes we had made with her as she left the room.

The next evening after my late shift there was a knock on my bedroom door and there Ellen stood with a huge grin on her face and a lovely little tete a tete plant in her hand." Can I come in Leah?" she asked eagerly. I knew she had come to a conclusion about her relationship with Michael. I beckoned her in and we sat on the bed.

"I can't thank you enough for helping me sort my feelings out. Michael and I have finished for good. I told him in no uncertain terms that I don't come second to anyone and I don't date men who two time me."

"Good for you Ellen. That's a strong positive attitude. I'm proud of you" I said.

She gave me the pretty little plant as a 'thank you' together with a little peck on the cheek.

"And I didn't even break down when I told him " she said.

"Anyway," I said, "I thought that you were getting on well with Phil at Jessica's party on New Year's Eve?

"No" she replied. "That was the effects of the drink. He's not for me. He's older than you think"

"Guess what too. Some fantastic news. You won't believe what happened" she said excitedly. "One of the Doctors at the hospital invited me out for a meal when I'm off next. He is someone that I have worked with and he has a wicked sense of humour."

"Awesome " I said " One door closes and another opens. I told you there were plenty more fish in the sea. Decent fish at that."

At work later in the week one of the nurses sidled up to me and said that she had heard on the grapevine that Dr. Taylor had got a soft spot for Ellen. He knew she was in a relationship with

Michael so he had waited and watched and as soon as he heard that her relationship was over had asked her for a date. News travels fast in the workplace, even between different hospitals a grapevine exists.

Let's hope this works out for Ellen. I crossed my fingers and made a wish. He sounded like a decent man.

That night I had a long conversation with my friend Lynne who sadly was still in her dead-end Blackpool job. I updated her with the latest news of my relationship, the engagement, the upset in Rishi's family and my deep feelings. "It sounds like he is the one for you. This could be your destiny. Like I have always said, your course in life is predetermined. It's something that is out of your hands. But to me it sounds like destiny has brought you two together." That was exactly what I wanted to hear.

CHAPTER 24

A Valentine surprise

I went to Rishi's bedsit flat in Tooting, South London to cook him a meal as he was on a weekend duty. I had gone to the supermarket on the way and picked up some pasta, tomatoes, basil and a strong Italian cheese. I had laid the table trying to make it look as good as possible. Single men in bedsits don't appear to have much in the way of dishes and utensils but somehow I would manage.

Rishi liked pasta so I busily prepared the dish for when he came in from the hospital. Rishi seemed excited when he arrived home. I was mystified why.

We sat down and while we chatted over a large glass of chilled prosecco Rishi told me that he had booked a Valentine surprise. "A three night getaway in Nice on the Cote d'Azur in the south of France." he told me. It was my turn to get excited then.

"First" he said "Lets check your rota or I'll have to take someone else" he joked. "I have had a look and I think I got it right."

Yes, all was well. Rishi was spot on. I was free. We would go next Wednesday, Thursday and return late on Friday in time for my weekend shift.

Rishi went on to explain that he had hired an Airbnb garden flat which was 50 metres from the seafront of Nice's Promenade Anglaise and right in the heart of the restaurant area. It was a good time to go as not only was it Valentines Day but it was also Mardi Gras in Nice. There were things happening close to our accommodation. He had also bought the two return plane tickets.

It was a lovely surprise. I hadn't been to Nice before, only to Paris when I was a schoolgirl, that long ago.

After our meal we took a look at the website advertising the Carnival. It looked like fun so we decided to go to the Nice Carnival Parade of Lights so Rishi booked online tickets.

Wednesday morning came and we found ourselves at Gatwick Airport in good time. We had small carry-on cases so went straight through, pausing at some of the perfumes and expensive after-shaves on our way. We boarded. The flight took off on time and we were airbourne. Less than two hours later we touched down at Nice Airport.

I couldn't believe that we had got there so quickly. One minute we were in chilly London and now in beautiful Nice with swaying palm trees lining the streets, well laid out flower beds and blue sunny skies.

Nice has a new tram from the Airport to town and we zoomed along checking our progress on a street map, making sure that we got off at the stop nearest our accomodation.

We made contact with the lady who serviced the flat and she met us with the key.

The apartment was delightful. There was everything that you needed for a three night stay. The soft comfortable bed was on an open floor above. "I feel like Heidi in Grandfathers Swiss cabin" I joked as I climbed the stairs to put some clothes away. I felt so happy.

That night we had a good walk round the beautiful town of Nice to get our bearings. We indulged in a huge shared Calzon Pizza at a restaurant set in the heart of the pedestrianised area.It was chilly once the sun went down but the flames from the restaurant heater warmed us through. The wine flowed and we chinked our glasses together as Rishi made a toast." To my Leah, the kindest, most caring girl who I will be spending the rest of my life with.You are my Valentine." We both had too much to drink but we didn't care. We were on holiday, deliriously happy and after all, it was Valentines Day.

Hanging onto each other to keep upright and slightly the worst for wear we made our way back to the apartment. We fell straight into bed for a good night's sleep so we could make the most of our day tomorrow. Life felt good.

CHAPTER 25

Bad news

We woke up next morning suddenly with the sound of Rishi's mobile phone ringing. It was almost 7 in the morning. A bit early to get a call. It was Archan, Rishi's brother calling from Mumbai. Something must be wrong I reasoned.

True enough Archan told Rishi that their father had been taken to a Jaipur hospital. He had felt very unwell and was in great pain. He needed tests.

"Oh no. said Rishi. Is it his heart?" Rishi had turned quite pale and was looking to sit down with the shock.

Archan said that he had no clear idea what was wrong as tests were being carried out. He hadn't actually seen his father face to face as he was still at his workplace in Mumbai. Archan had spoken to his father on the phone. His father has said that he didn't want Rishi to be informed of the illness as he couldn't forgive him for backing out of the arranged marriage.

Archan, being on Rishi's side of the argument anyway, had ignored his fathers wishes and made the call to let Rishi know the situation.

Recently Rishi had tried to phone his father a couple of times to patch things up but his father had put the phone down on him.

Archan thought that his father was being ridiculous but said that we all needed to understand and recognise that his father was from a different generation.

Rishi asked Archan if there was anything he could do for his father. He explained that we were away in Nice for a couple of days. This news had come at a bad time as Rishi felt that Jaipur was a long way away and to complicate things we were not even at home.

Archan assured us that he would let us know of any developments. His father was in his early seventies even though Rishi thought he didn't look his age.

At the end of the conversation Rishi asked Archan to tell his father that he wanted to thank him for being a good father to him and that he loved him very much. Archan said he would pass on the message. He was flying from Mumbai to Jaipur later that day to see his father at the hospital. Rishi had felt that he could do no more at that time.

The news had put a dark cloud over our mini break but we decided to await Archan's update and try to put his faher's illness at the back of our minds for the momen,t as best we could.

Our tickets for the Carnival Parade was that same night so we had all day to ourselves. We had a local guide book and discussed how to get the most out of the day.The sun was shining and it was like spring. Much warmer than London even though it was only February
"St Paul de Vence sounds a good place to go to" said Rishi. We hopped on a local bus for about an hours journey to this most beautiful fortified village. It was a town where many artists had made their home and it still had about three hundred people living inside its strong stone walls to this day.

An exuberant tourist stopped for a chat in the sunshine. He had heard our English accents. He told us that Bill Wyman, the bassist from the Rolling Stone lived there and that many stars and personalities from bygone days had made their home there too. The Russian born Jewish artist Marc Chagall, noted for his cubist artwork had lived there for many years and was in fact buried in the peaceful St Paul de Vence graveyard.

Rishi looked the artist up on his 'phone. "Chagalls most famous painting is probably' I and the village' which hangs in a New York gallery." Rishi informed me.

Apparently St Paul de Vence has over two million visitors a year and no wonder, as it is certainly an unusual and beautiful place with a history. It has something for both young and old. We followed a sloping uphill footpath. Flowers made from small stones were set into the footpath making it very unusual and special. We walked in and out of the little arty shops stopping here and there wondering at the originality of the wide range of artworks using many different mediums. We passed ancient fountains, gateways and porches and sat awhile in a shady ancient square taking in the beauty of this historic walled town. It was such a romantic spot.

Eventually we came to some steps leading up to the most wonderful views of the hills and snow capped mountains. "I think that this is the most romantic place that I have ever been to" said Rishi. I had to agree.

Naturally we kissed and held hands. Happily we made our way to an open air restaurant that nestled in the fortress walls. We dined on local freshly caught poached fish served in a wild mushroom sauce. An apple cake topped with a dusting of icing sugar and toasted almonds followed. "This is the dessert for our wedding reception. Delicious" Rishi joked.

Following such a special lunch we headed off with our arms around each other, back to the bus stop to return to Nice, mindful that we had tickets for the evening Carnival.

Early in the evening we sent a text to Archan to ask how Rishi's father was doing and if he had any test results. Jaipu, where his father was in hospital was ahead of Nice by a time difference of four and a half hours. We needed to hear from him soon as it was already the evening and wouldn't be too long before Archan may be going to bed. An hour went past without hearing any news and so Rishi decided to phone Archan himself to check progress. Nervously he awaited for Archan to answer.

It was relatively good news. Archan had been told by the Doctor that the diagnosis was gallstones which is far less serious than the suspected heart problem. Archan explained that they were keeping his father in and he would have an operation that night as he was still in great pain. The staff were apparently getting him ready as we spoke. It was a routine operation with no complications expected.

"Phew. At least it's not his heart." Rishi said, relieved. "I would hate it and never forgiven myself if my father had died of a heart attack and we hadn't made peace over the arranged marriage and family upset."

I phoned Mum to tell her about Rishi's father and about the wonderful time we were having in Nice. "I knew you would love Nice, Your Dad and I went there when we were first married. Sounds like you are having a great time, the pair of you." said Mum. "So glad that Rishi's father has his diagnosis. You never know what is round the corner. Modern medicine and treatment is wonderful these days."

There was nothing more that we could do other than to send his father our best wishes through Archan. Better to wait until after the imminent operation to speak to his father and maybe there would be a chance to make up the disagreement.

Now time to enjoy ourselves at the Carnival Parade of Lights. It began at nine o'clock so we wrapped up warm to keep out the cold as the sun had gone down. Hand in hand we set off to the magical Place Massena where we would view the parade.

CHAPTER 26

Mardi Gras-Nice Style

The Mardi Gras Carnival Parade of Lights was no disappointment. Mardi Gras, translated means Fat Tuesday. The date varies depending on when Easter falls. In Nice it takes the form of an exuberant parade. A different theme is adopted each year and for this Mardi Gras the theme was King of Cinema.

We took our seats and waited, not quite sure what to expect. There were a lot of people of every age in fancy dress adding to the atmosphere. Fancy dress had been encouraged and it allowed free entry to the parade.

The crowd were whipped up into a frenzy by a youth group of talented acrobats who kept everyone entertained as they did back flips, somersaults, danced and twizzled their partners in the air. They sparkled in their leotards and skin tight pants as they were thrown around with such skill. "Can you do that Leah?" Rishi laughed. They were amazing. Spotlights raced up and down the aisles of onlookers and large television screens helped everyone to get better views of the parade. As it started confetti canons were set off. Nobody could escape the tiny paper shapes as they dropped from above, floating down like snow into our hair and clothing and laying like a carpet underfoot. I'd never seen anything like it. To add to the experience children with cans of silly string were enjoying spraying it at anyone and anything. The atmosphere was happy and it was lovely to see lots of families sharing in the fun.

The procession featured stars from the silver screen. Marilyn Monroe, Stan Laurel and Oliver Hardy were depicted on huge carnival floats. Comical caricatures of politicians and the President of France were abundant. Bollywood was represented by a huge life-sized beautifully decorated mechanical elephant which had an Indian man in full costume and a turban riding high on the elephants back. Huge colourful and comical papier mache puppets walked along the parade, each with someone inside peering out of a small gap to breathe. There were musical bands and dancers snaking rhythmically along the procession route, everyone giving one hundred per cent.

Rishi spotted a huge blue float of Ganesh, the popular deity who has an elephant head and a human body. He explained that Ganesh is a forerunner of success and a destroyer of obstacles that could get in the way.

The float was beautiful and as it slowly passed us I reconnected with my desire to go to India one day and experience first hand the history and culture.

It had been a brilliant evening and as we slowly wandered hand in hand through the streets littered with party paraphernalia to our apartment I realised how lucky I was to have had this Mardi Gras opportunity. It is something everyone should have on their bucket list .

Thank you Rishi. Love you with all my heart.

CHAPTER 27

Menton for the Day

We woke up early, popped to the local supermarket and feasted on some fresh crusty French bread from the local shop with delicious jam and coffee, followed by a Pain au Chocolat each. "Naughty but nice." I said to Rishi. "We deserve it with the stress of the operation"

He checked his phone anxiously. Archan was returning to Mumbai where he had a flat and an office, part of his fathers company. There was no message so after breakfast Rishi gave him a call. "Hi Bro" said Archan. "I was going to call you but was aware of the time difference so didn't want to wake you on your holidays. I saw Dad before I hopped on a flight back to Mumbai. Dad was a bit sleepy but not in pain. Apparently it had all gone to plan. I would have stayed with him longer but I needed to get back to work to keep the family business ticking over. He went on to say that his father was now on a ward and his wife, their mother, Sharmila, was by his side. The operation had been done by keyhole surgery so it was less invasive with a shorter recovery time. We both felt a sense of relief. "No operation is 100% safe and when you are in your seventies it is more serious than in someone younger." I told him. I reassured Rishi that gall bladder surgery is a common problem and that complete recovery was usually the outcome. "Phew," said Rishi with a sigh of relief. "He just needs recovery time."

"Well, now let us make the most of our time left in Nice before we catch our late flight. I have been reading about a lemon festival in Menton which is down the coast, past Monaco." "Great idea" I said keenly. "We need to make the most of our last day. I'll be ready in five." I cleared up the breakfast dishes and quickly put on a bit of make up.

Off we set to catch a bus from Nice port. We had to do a little bit of walking but it was through a lovely child friendly park with a huge climbing frame in the form of a whale and a water feature which was spouting and dancing up and down randomly." Great for kids." I thought. Even the adults were chancing their luck as they tried to dodge the fountains. Though it was only February it was another bright day.

Buses to Menton were frequent and we were lucky enough to get a seat so that we could follow the most beautiful coastline." It reminds me of the Amalfi coast in southern Italy." I told Rishi. He had never been there himself. "We shall go one day" Rishi replied." You can show me round." So that was India, Hungary and southern Italy on our list already and we had only recently been engaged. The bus ride was amazing. Luxury homes were perched high above us and sometimes below us too. The sea was never far from sight and it was a deep blue green catching a reflection from the cloudless sky. We were so lucky to have weather like this. "This bit of brighness makes such a difference and to experience it in February is so special" I whispered to Rishi.
Once at Menton we walked along the seafront and sat on the beach for a while catching the warmth and watching the waves. "Do you know Leah? I love the south of France. The natural light is wonderful. Everything looks so bright." He was right. The light did something special for colour. "It is why artists love this area." I said.

On some of the days Menton had hosted a Lemon Parade with floats bedecked with oranges and lemons. But on this day the main attraction was a garden full of different exhibits depicting well known folk stories. The static displays were imaginatively made from oranges and lemons and were an unbelievable sight. Some were eight metres high. One exhibit had moving parts with witches swinging round and all were just amazing. We sat in this garden and Rishi got some information about this annual treat which is apparently an internationally renown event. Google told us that the first lemon tree supposedly took root at Menton. It was planted by Eve of the Adam and Eve duo.

We bought some scented lemon soap from one of the small stalls and stopped for a lemon pancake at another. "Pancakes are associated with Mardi Gras." I told Rishi. "A way of using up your flour, eggs and milk before you go on more frugal food during Lent." Rishi nodded knowingly. Although he had been born in India spending the majority of his life in England he was familiar with lots of customs.
We took lots of photographs so that we could show our friends this unusual celebration and sent Mum a WhatsApp of the pair of us standing next to a life sized Indian elephant made from oranges. Hard to imagine but perfectly true.

"We had better get a move on back now. Collect our cases and catch the flight home" said Rishi, eyeing his watch. So off we went, back to Nice feeling smug that we had managed to fit in this extra day and brilliant experience. We sped off to the airport on the tram, catching the last plane of the day back to Gatwick Airport. This Valentine trip had been great fun and together we had many memories to share.

Rishi stayed at mine overnight as it was late when we got back. Luckily my weekend shift the next day was lates. A chance for a lie-in and recuperate from our action packed wonderful mini break.

CHAPTER 28

Life goes on

Life went on as normal once back at work. It was busy, hard work and at times stressful.

In Orthopaedics the patients are often feeling quite well, except for their broken bones, as opposed to other wards where patients are feeling physically ill. Patients can be brilliant, especially the ones who have been injured through sport, football, rugby and such like. They get everyone laughing with their teasing and banter.

On my day off I called Mum and we spoke for ages. She totally surprised me by telling me of an unexpected message that she had received through Facebook. It was Phil from the shared house. He asked Mum if she would like to meet up for a meal.

Mum didn't know what it was about but had agreed to meet Phil for lunch. Phil had suggested The Pavilion Cafe in Avenham Park, Preston, about fifteen miles from Mum's home town of Blackpool. I hadn't heard anything from Phil since the Christmas party at our house. I felt intrigued about his request for lunch. I wondered what he had in mind travelling up to Lancashire. "Mum, you must let me know what it was all about when you have met" I said.

Next we chatted at length about Rishi's father and the breakdown of the relationship with him. "Well these things happen" she said wisely and went on to say that often in this type of breakdown the love for one's son and the family bond will come through in the end. "Hopefully that will happen." I said. Mum was usually right........

Mum said that she really wanted to see us again as soon as possible and she would like to treat us to a romantic celebration meal but I explained that my holiday allowance wouldn't allow any more time off as Rishi had suggested that we have a holiday in India in the near future. All my holidays had to be saved for that. "Wow, that sounds really exciting Leah" Mum said. "India, who'd have ever thought."

That night Rishi told me that at the beginning of last week he had written a letter to his father and sent it first class to his parent's flat in Jaipur. The letter had been put in a new envelope and immediately returned to Rishi unopened. He had just received it today.

I don't think Rishi had expected this reaction. In the letter Rishi had wished his father a speedy recovery and apologised for the upset he had caused. As Rishi's father had not opened the letter we would never know the heartfelt apology inside.

On receiving the returned letter Rishi had immediately telephoned his mother. The housekeeper had answered the phone and told his mother that Rishi was calling. She had refused to take the call. "Madam is not accepting your call" the housekeeper said, with attitude, before slamming the phone down.

I could tell that Rishi was very hurt. "We have each other" I said trying to comfort him." I'm sure that we can put things right in time."

I had an idea. At the Nice Carnival Rishi had pointed out Ganesh, the deity who had an elephant head and a rotund human body. Ganesh was noted for the ability to solve difficult problems whilst taking away obstacles. These were just the qualities that Rishi needed at this time. The very next day I went to Tooting Market where I found a stall selling Hindu replicas of Ganesh. I took it to Rishi's empty flat as a gesture and surprise, hoping it would help him to overcome the problems he was having with his family.

That night I received a text message.

'Thank you for Ganesh. He is helping me with the family problem. Love you forever' it read and by the side were two emoji love hearts.

CHAPTER 29

What a surprise

Mum called me unexpectedly for one of our Skype catch-up chats. She sounded a bit worried about meeting up with Phil. "Oh. Mum. Why didn't you message him back and ask what he was doing in Preston." I said. She replied that she hadn't wanted to appear nosey. Typical Mum.

All day long it got to me. Perhaps he had a job interview, maybe he was on holiday or even on a conference. I'd have to wait to find out but all the same it was niggling me.

Mum had asked me what I thought that she should wear. Phil was a casual laid-back person, so not to get too dressed up, I suggested. A pair of trousers and a nice jumper should tick the box I advised, thinking of what I remembered of his casual style. "Wrap up warm. There's chilly winds about" I warned. "Let me know how you get on."

The next day came and went. I was rushed off my feet at work dealing with some complicated problems on the ward and lots of new patients. Mum's meet-up had gone from my mind but that evening, quite late, the phone rang and it was Mum. She said that she had had a super day and had only just got in. Phil had met her in Avalon Park, as planned. They had lunch in the cafe and then a good long walk round the park. They went to see the Japanese garden too. It was a bit early in the year to see any park at its best but Mum said that there was lots of signs of the end of winter. They had walked into Preston and found a nice pub where they had sat and chatted over a drink and warmed themselves up. Over three hours later, yes, over three hours later, they had left the pub and Phil had taken Mum to dinner in the swanky hotel near the park where they had had a superb meal, wine and enjoyed the rich, luxurious decor and atmosphere.

"OK. Sounds like you had a great time. But what on earth was Phil doing in Preston?" I queried. Mum told me that Phil had felt bored and frustrated in his current job. He had a bit of money tucked away and so had decided to take a year out and do a Masters Degree that related to his career and The University of Lancashire offered a suitable course called 'Music Industry, Management and Promotion.'

Phil didn't know Lancashire and wanted to see if it was to be his number one choice. He would be moving into the area where his Uni was situated. Mum said, "He was simply looking me up. We got on really well and he was really relaxed and friendly. Remember when we went to the Science Museum and Harrods and Phil came along with us? We got on like a house on fire then too. He is a really interesting person once he puts his guard down. Anyway, Phil is looking around other Uni's and has to apply as a mature student. If he gets in one of the Uni's he will start next Autumn, in October. He's quite determined."
That was the end of the conversation as it was late and it had been a long day. It was good to hear Mum so animated and that Phil had treated her well. He was a deep person but quite a gent I recalled   .

The next day I had another surprise. Excitedly Rishi met me with a huge hug. "Leah. We are off to India" he said, grabbing my arm. "I have made enquiries about flights and accommodation. We can go to Jaipur without telling my parents and then we can call on them unexpectedly. I really want you to meet them and get all this family breakdown nonsense out of the way."

My immediate thought was would I need any injections? We laughed at that. That was the nurse in me over-thinking medical thoughts. "Will I need a Visa? When were you thinking of going?"

Coincidentally I had just heard that day about my annual leave enquiry. The answer had come just at the right time. I had fourteen days annual leave owing.

Before I knew it Rishi had sorted out the Visa requirements, booked the flights, a hotel and sent me off to the Doctors to get some necessary injections.
One piece of good news was that Rishi had received a long email from Anneka. She was back from Australia. Her visit, looking after the elderly relative, had gone on longer than expected. She apologised for not contacting Rishi earlier. Anneka said she was aware that she needed to speak to Rishi's parents to give her side of the arranged marriage saga. She said that she would be contacting Sharmila and Pradeep, Rishi's parents really soon. She said that she knew exactly what to say.

Rishi sounded relieved. "Whatever the outcome, we have tried" he said.

We were travelling in mid-March for two weeks, allowing plenty of time to rest, relax and for sightseeing. Thoughtful Rishi had coincided our trip with the Hindu Holi which is a big celebration, like Christmas in England. We would also be able to see the Elephant Festival that I had heard so much about. "Two big things on my bucket list." I told Mum.
Cool, calm and collected Rishi had all the answers. He was such a catch. I was so lucky to have him in my life. The next couple of weeks whizzed past and I became more and more excited.

Rishi printed off the boarding passes. We needed to be at the airport in good time for the British Airways 20.45 flight that arrived next day in Jaipur, capital of Rajasthan in northern India, at 12.55 having stopped off at Delhi where we needed to change planes. It all sounded so exciting. It was my first long-haul trip.

At the earliest opportunity I took myself off to Primark for some new clothes. I had checked out the average temperatures for Jaipur in March and was elated to see that it was between 23 and 31 degrees Celsius. At night the average temperature was about 15C, so a comfortable night-time climate.

I love the sun and getting a nice tan so I headed towards the sundresses. I reminded myself that I needed to cover up a bit for modesty in India so I bought some floral baggy trousers and striped slacks, a few new cotton tops and a blouse. It was a great Primark spree. Luckily the summer stock had recently arrived and I managed to buy several colourful and fashionable items at a good price. I would have liked a new swimsuit but money was just a bit short for that.I would need spending money for trips and suchlike.

Once home I started packing my case as time was of the essence. I put my very best dress in carefull in case we went anywhere special. It was turquoise soft chiffon dress that I had bought last year for a friends wedding. It would be important to look just right if I got the chance to meet Rishi's parents. That is if they come round and are willing to adjust to our situation.

CHAPTER 30

India, here we come

It was great to be going to India and if we could mend the relationship between Rishi and his parents it would be a bonus.

Rishi had told me that his mother was a bit of a diva, loved to keep up with the Jones' and was keen on family values and tradition. His father was apparently quiet, strict and a man of his word. Just occasionally he lost his temper. "Quite a duo to contend with" I whispered to myself.

As the arranged marriage to Anneka wasn't going ahead I wondered how I would be received. Maybe I'd be blamed? Perhaps they would hold the past against me? Maybe his parents would accept Rishi but not me?

I felt worried about the situation but just had to wait and see what would happen. We couldn't predict what reception we would get. It might even be that Rishi is rejected for ever and he never saw his parents again.

So our break to India was tinged with anticipation. I kept my thoughts to myself. If I tell Rishi it would upset him. Thank goodness I was a strong woman and didn't break down snivelling at every difficulty that I faced in life. Together, Rishi and I were a sturdy pair and nothing was going to get between us.
Soon the big getaway day came round. Excitedly we made our way on the London Underground to Heathrow Airport for our flight to India. We had allowed more than enough time, setting off at three in the afternoon to allow for any hold-ups. It can get very busy round Heathrow and it is a massive airport.

We would be ahead of the rush hour plus I didn't want the stress of being late. Rishi helped me with my heavy suitcase.

"Leah, I'll take that" he said caringly. He knew that I had minor back problems due to lifting badly at work. Luckily we found lifts and escalators to help us so it wasn't too difficult and our new bright red suitcases had four wheels making it easier to manoeuvre them. I carried our two light holdalls containing items we might need on the journey.... wipes for a freshen up, a warm jumper each, as it could get cold on the journey and some magazines.

The flight to Delhi went well. Rishi chatted to the friendly man sitting next to him. They shared a few laughs and life experiences. I settled down with my magazines. We both watched a film on the in-flight entertainment. This all helped to pass the six and a half hour journey. Once nightfall came and the lights dimmed we held hands and fell into a light sleep, me resting my head on Rishi's strong shoulder. It had been a long day.
I awoke from my sleep with a start. I looked lovingly at Rishi. I knew just by being at his side that he was the love of my life. I reflected on how things had changed since I left my Blackpool hometown. It had taken a bit of time and adjustment to live in London. It was so busy, people rushing about everywhere, all colours and religions. I had made lots of new friends and acquaintances. Fortunately, I loved both, my hospital job and living in the shared house and I was grateful for the strength this gave me. The best of all was that I had fallen in love. It had been more than I ever thought possible to feel the way I did, and here I was now. Little old me, a Lancashire nurse excitedly on my way to Jaipur, India. It didn't seem real. My life had certainly moved up a notch.

Once at Delhi, we waited for our connecting flight for the final leg which was just one hour, landing in Jaipur at one 'o clock in the afternoon.
Due to the time difference and a journey of nearly twelve hours we were pleased to find a sunny, hot vibrant city greeting us. "I love it already and I love you too" I whispered to Rishi.

A welcome taxi took us the short ride to the spectacular pink building that was our plush hotel, right in the town centre. We fell into bed and slept until we needed sleep no more.

CHAPTER 31

A taste of tradition

The next day dawned and Rishi and I went down to breakfast. We felt refreshed and had got over the long flight. "It wasn't too bad, was it, Leah? I hoped that you wouldn't find your first really long flight too much." "No, I enjoyed it especially falling asleep on your shoulder. You make a lovely pillow" I laughed.

We had a long chat with an older couple sitting at the next table. They introduced themselves as Monica and Guy. Both were loud and gregarious. They had come from New York to see the Holi Festival. Jaipur was apparently one of the best places to see what went on. "We have heard all about it and I said to my wife Monica, lets go and see it for ourselves. So here we are, all ready to see the Holi fires and the Festival of Colour. Apparently they say elephant parade is spectacular too."

It turned out that the couple, Monica and Guy, were second time round honeymooners. We arranged to join up with them to go to the Elephant Festival which was on later that day.

"You can explain all about the different customs as this is your hometown Rishi" said Guy, the American gentleman," as he patted Rishi on the back. "Delighted to" said Rishi.

I asked Rishi to explain what the Holi Festival represented. "The festival of Holi happens every year when Hindu's celebrate the end of winter and welcomes the new spring."Rishi said knowingly. "Its name comes from a wicked witch called Holika who lost her life in a fire. Holi is celebration of good over evil. It is a very old story from the Hindu scriptures" Rishi added "There are lots of Hindu stories that help people to make sense of their faith in an easier form."

That got me thinking about the different upbringings that

Rishi and I had experienced. Although Rishi had been schooled in England from a very young child he had also experienced the Hindu cultures and way of life. It was like leading a double life, a dual identity of different values, customs and experiences.

Above all, one thing that was important to us both was family. We had discussed family values many times. On an occasion like Holi our family should be together and not be split by an argument as was the case..

Monica, Guy's wife, dripping with expensive jewellery and hosting long red painted fingernails seemed thrilled to have met us.
"You two actually met each other in London?" she said amazed. "Yes," Leah told her. "It's not unusual as London is a melting pot for all nationalities."
Monica was a lovely lady, intent on making the most of her time in India after a few sad years when she had been widowed. That was until Guy had come into her life. "He has been wonderful for me" she drawled. "I call him my knight in shining armour for coming to my rescue."

The hotel Reception desk held all the information needed about these annual celebrations. The famous elephant parade was to take place on the eve of Holi. The Receptionist advised where to go to see the best Holi bonfire. These bonfires were wood fires with an effigy of Holika the wicked witch on top. It was a bit like Guy Fawkes in the UK. Apparently some people wiped the ashes from the Holi fire onto their bodies as a form of purification.

We took a leaflet about The Festival of Colours which was on the main day of Holi. It was a celebration where adults and children would throw highly coloured powders, called gulal at each other."We are lucky to be here at this time " I said, "to experience the most important festival in India."

Later that day as arranged Monica and Guy met up with us to

share a taxi to the Elephant Festival. We were soon laughing and joking as if we had been friends for years.

The Elephant Festival, put on by the Rajasthan Government was unbelievable. There was a traditional procession with lots of huge elephants who's heads had been lovingly painted with bright coloured patterns and flowers. On their massive feet they wore thick elephant bracelets of silver. Even their massive legs were ornately hand-painted. Some elephants wore silver head-dresses which glistened in the afternoon sun. On their backs were rich embellished velvet coats bedecked with silver em-broidery. Huge, colourful silk scarves hung from their ears. Each elephant had a master sitting on top, smartly turned out in an expensive white silk suit embroidered with silver thread. The masters sported large red impressive turbans. Some elephants even carried two men, one holding a massive fringed umbrella over the main master. There were men riding mock horses, ra-ther like ornate hobby horses with golden heads. Bands were playing a host of unusual shiny instruments as their drummers kept time. An abundance of flags, tassels, turbans, twirling sil-ver rods, singing and dancing, children, folk dancers and witch doctors completed the spectacle. What a beautiful experience. "We are so lucky to be part of this" Monica gushed. "For you, baby, anything" smiled Guy, as he looked lovingly at his new wife. Rishi caught my eye and gave me a wink.

A couple of hours passed and we followed up with a visit to a huge Holi bonfire celebrating the casting out winter, wel-coming the spring, good over evil, forgiving and forgetting and repairing broken relationships. " My parents should take these values on board" said Rishi. "After all the Holika fires are about repairing broken relationships." "Perhaps they will" I said hope-fully.
It was a really crowded affair, hot and bustling. You could sense the excitement. There was lots of laughter from local Jaipurians as they participated fully in their festival. Many were dancing round the fire singing loudly, whilst others took the opportun-

ity to perform religious rituals. Such a great sense of celebration. It was a wonderful, unusual evening,
In the bar back at the hotel we chatted effortlessly to Guy and Monica. We all agreed that we shouldn't drink too much or burn the midnight oil as the following day we had to be up early. After all, it was the Festival of Colour. Gulal, a vibrant highly coloured cornflower powder, found in every bright shade imaginable was ready for throwing, all to celebrate Holi. We had enjoyed such an exciting day and had more to come tomorrow.

Once in bed Rishi and I discussed the best way to approach his parents about the impasse. "Let's enjoy tomorrow and then face my parents once Holi is over. I think I will ring them and tell the Housekeeper that I am in town and want to make a time to see them. See what happens." he said casually. It was almost as if he wasn't letting the situation bother him. I knew that was just bravado. Knowing Rishi so well I knew that he was desperate to make amends.

With that decided we kissed goodnight and Rishi went to sleep. I lay there thinking about our day. The new friends we had made, the unique Elephant Festival, the gentle proud Indian people, the beautiful buildings in Jaipur, the vibrant city colours, the sparkling sunlight, the warmth of the climate and the way that this beautiful city was alive, chaotic and bustling. What a stunning country.

More experiences tomorrow I thought as I drifted off into a deep sleep.

CHAPTER 32

The Holi Festival

We had a chat to the Receptionist about today's Rangwali Festival of Colour. "The streets will be alive with music. Bands will be playing round town and outside the temples. There will be huge drums and music. Some youngsters will have water fights and they will chase each other and play fight. It will certainly be a free for all," said the graceful receptionist smiling. "You can stay in the hotel if you would rather. The hotel had put on its own Holi celebration for visitors who didn't feel up to venturing into the chaos of the streets"

After speaking with Monica and Guy we sensibly opted to join the hotel's celebration with the thought of perhaps joining the town's celebration later.

The hotel manager appeared. "Ladies and Gentlemen, Let the celebrations begin" he announced. We were each given some coconut oil to rub onto our skin and simple white T shirts to wear. We were told that this would make it easier to wash off the bright gulal powder and that the colour would show up better. We duly obliged.

Some of the hotel staff had been instructed to come onto the hotel rooftop with boxes of different fine coloured powders. There was quite a gathering of about sixty hotel guests, all game to take part in this bucket-list experience. Two Jaipurians in beautiful national costume appeared with their drums and the party got going. Gulal powder was being thrown at each and everyone of us from all directions, while the drums beat rhythmically. Strangers were hugging each other while shouting Happy Holi. The hotel guests really threw themselves into the spirit of the occasion. There was laughter from all directions as powders came whizzing towards us. A lot of photos and 'phone videos were taken to show the folks back home. Lots of shouting and laughter could be heard as the usually sedate hotel guests let their hair down. Before long we were covered, yellow, pink, green, purple, in fact all the colours that you can think of. The hotel rooftop floor was a rainbow of gulal powder.

Just as things were winding down trays of sparkling wine appeared and some sweet delicacies. Gajak a dry sesame seed treat and some Mava Kochori, pastry pieces with nuts, cardamom and nutmeg. We feasted both on this unique experience and the unusual and delicious hotel treats.

"Wow" said Monica in her New York drawl. "That was great fun. I read about this festival and always wanted to see it." Guy, a jolly type, swallowed his champagne and went for seconds. "This is great but I won't be venturing onto the streets. I'm a bit too old for all that. See you folks later. I'm going for a shower to wash off the gulal. Its gone everywhere," Guy said with a cheeky smile. "It was worth it to be part of the fun." If you two are around later perhaps we could play a few games of cards and share the evening?"

Later that day Rishi and I decided that we wanted to experience the festivities in town so we put on clean clothes and oiled ourselves up again just in case. The town was its usual chaotic self. Motorbikes with three abreast were winding their way through the narrow streets. Choking coaches had brought in streams of visitors to witness the event so tourists were everywhere. Here and there cows ambled unmolested in traffic-choked streets. The cows, of course are sacred, worshipped animal to Hindus. Someone had even decorated the cows for the Holi festival and they wandered the streets oblivious that this was a special and very different day. Cars hooted in traffic jams and the sun shone. Everywhere you went people were covered in many shades of gulal. There was a lot of general merrymaking. By this time of day alcohol had been a contributing factor to the mayhem in town. We wandered round the walled pink city hand in hand wishing people Happy Holi, ourselves once again covered in gulal powder and relishing this experience. We were so lucky to have seen this annual spectacle.

Back at the hotel, washed and brushed we discussed the situation with Rishi's parents. Rishi suddenly took the bull by the horns and picked up his phone. He made the call. The housekeeper answered and he told the housekeeper that it was imperative that he spoke to his parents. She scuttled off and next minute his mother came to the phone.
" Hello Mum. Happy Holi. I am here in Jaipur with my fiancé, Leah. We would love to meet up with you and maybe talk things over? How is my father? I hope that he is recovering from his operation and that you are well too? Mum, I want you to know that you mean so much to me and I do not want to lose you or my father in my life."

He waited for a response, unsure of thre reaction he'd get. His mother had gone quiet. All of a sudden she began to speak a well thought-out response. It was almost as if she had planned out what to say if the occasion ever arose. "Rishi, you are my first born and much loved son. Your father and I have discussed the situation and the arranged marriage over and over again. We have realised that when we sent you for your education to England you became an Englishman in so many ways. We respect this and can see how you want to follow your heart. Last week Anneka arranged to visit us. She explained that she has someone else in her life too so perhaps what has happened is destiny.

Anneka has told us that she is deeply in love and she feels that her father would have approved of her new fiancé. He is reported to be quite wealthy so her father would think that she had chosen well.

Your father and I have realised that sometimes things don't work out as planned. We are a bit old fashioned and stuck in our ways, which accounts for the way we reacted when you explained that you were not going through with the marriage to

Anneka."

Rishi looked happy, like a weight had been lifted off his shoulders. "And how is my Father." he asked. "Completely recovered except that he has to be careful with eating spicy food." She laughed. "Not quite the thing for a spice business man. He is enjoying a quiet Holi in his own special way."

"Will you come for dinner tomorrow?" said his mother. "We would love to meet Leah and welcome her into our family. Seven o'clock sharp." she said.

So all the worry and perplexing was lifted if Sharmila, his mother, was true to her word. She sounded like she wasn't blaming me and that she would accept me to be Rishi's wife. Hopefully she wouldn't hold a grudge. After all, I was just the piggy in the middle and all I had done was to fall deeply in love with her son. We would go tomorrow evening and then we would know for sure.

I thought it strange that Rishi's mother had mentioned that what had happened was destiny. Just that day I had been thinking about my Blackpool friend Lynne. I decided to send her an email. I described what we had been doing while on holiday here in India. The Elephant Festival, the Holi bonfire, the Festival of Colour with the gulal powder, the vibrant colours and the beautiful setting of Jaipur.

Unexpectedly I immediately received a reply from Lynne telling me that she had been drawn towards reading my stars in the local newspaper that very day and felt that she knew that I'd be in contact.

"It was a strange feeling that came over me" said Lynne. I knew I had to look at the regular stars prediction in the newspaper.

It read

'Much of your life has seemed more under the control of others but

that will now begin to change.
You will be in a much better position to work towards future goals
involving far reaching changes.'

Could this mean that Rishi and I had regained control of our lives? What could the far reaching changes mean? What future goals? Is this all just a coincidences?

Lynne had signed off with her usual comment that my life was already planned and I needed to believe.

"Maybe there is some truth in all this I wondered"......

That same evening was light-hearted after the day's festivities. We had a great time with Monica and Guy. They were great company, especially after a few drinks. Guy had a few card tricks up his sleeve,we told our unique stories and generally laughed a lot. A great evening.Happy Holi.

CHAPTER 33

Meeting the in-laws

We chilled out the next day booking tours for our remaining days and enjoying the rooftop garden, now back to its old self following the Holi celebration. Not a sign of gulal anywhere.

I needed to make a good impression tonight when meeting Rishi's parents. I checked my dress had survived the journey and picked out a pair of sparkly low heels to wear. I washed and conditioned my hair and took extra care with my make up, trying not to over do it. Rishi ordered the taxi for 6.30. By late afternoon I was ready so I Skyped my Mum to let her know our news.

Mum was really pleased to hear that Rishi's parents had come to terms with our relationship. Excitedly I told her about Jaipur, the pink city, its architecture, how we had booked to go to the monkey temple, Amer Fort, the former residence of Maharajas and the camel ride that Rishi had promised me.

"Sounds a wonderful experience Leah. Good Luck meeting Rishi's parents. I'm sure they will love you" she said.

I felt a bit nervous in the taxi but then who wouldn't. "Leah". I told myself "You are a strong independent woman. You are going to be an asset to this family."
The housekeeper showed us in. She wasn't very welcoming which unnerved me a little. The flat was very spacious and situated in the very best area of Jaipur. We were taken into the sitting room where his parents sat anticipating our arrival. Overhead fans were twirling keeping the air moving in the hot evening.

Rishi gave his parents a kiss on each cheek and a hug. I moved forward awkwardly not knowing what to expect. His mother took my hand and squeezed it. "So happy to meet you Leah. Let us be good friends. I have always wanted a daughter and you are the next best thing. Come, take a seat." she said as she looked me firmly in the eye. I shook his fathers hand and gave a nod of respect before sitting down on a large comfy chair. It hadn't been such a difficult meeting after all.

Both parents had come to terms that it was either lose Rishi or accept his choice of a wife.

A wonderful meal was served and we talked and drank telling of our adventures and all about our work, my family, my education and family values.
I knew that Rishi had come from a wealthy privileged family and it was evident. The home was beautifully furnished and his mother, Sharmila was dressed expensively in a deep golden brocade sari embellished with gold and silver threads. She wore it with a thick gold necklace that must have been worth a mint. She was a beautiful woman for her age and Rishi favoured her looks. Pradeep, his father looked distinguished and well dressed in a costly looking kurta, a kind of jacket and a pair of churidars, a form of trouser that went to his ankles and fell like bangles due to their length. He looked wise but a little formidable and strict with his greying hair and fine moustache.

I need not have worried about this meeting after all. Rishi's parents accepted me. I could tell that they liked the fact that I had a degree and a profession. In conversation they were delighted to hear that Rishi had been promoted at work and was thinking of getting on the property ladder. Ambition and success were high on their agendas.

They were interested to hear about my home town of Blackpool and that my mother held a responsible position at the National Savings offices and was in fact in charge of her section. It was obvious to me that although they were very kind, ambition and achievement were really important.
At the end of the evening Rishi's father spoke. "We are very

pleased to have met you Leah. The love that you have for each other is obvious. Welcome to our family."

We left their flat for the hotel. We felt that I had passed the first stage of their approval with flying colours. In the taxi home we both got the giggles. Rishi realised that his mother was quite a snob but I had held my own. "You did well Leah. The profession and the degree did the trick" Rishi said laughing. We invited Rishi's parents, Sharmila and Pradeep, for a meal later in the week at out hotel. Archan was apparently in Jaipur so we had invited him to join us.

His mother arrived at the hotel, again looking gorgeous in a traditional bright blue rich silk sari with her long black hair intricately arranged in a fancy bun style and secured with diamante pins. A different, but equally expensive looking bejewelled necklace hung around her neck.

It was great to meet Archan in the flesh and not on the phone as happened in Nice. He was certainly a handsome young man dressed in traditional Rajasthan clothing and looking well groomed. Soon it was like these brothers had never been apart. They chatted and told each other about the latest events in their lives. Laughter filled the air and I knew that there was a bond here that absence couldn't ignore.

As I had expected the subject of our future wedding cropped up. Rishi's parents had been to England a couple of times to see Rishi when he was at an expensive boarding school in Somerset. They had never seen the north of England and all its beauty. We decided then and there that we should get married in England and that they should come over for a Civil ceremony style wedding at Blackpool, my hometown. That would certainly be a different experience for them.

It was obvious that they had already discussed their proposed trip before our meeting. His parents expressed an interest in making their trip into a longer holiday. They wanted to see London with all the famous sights that they had heard about and seen in films and on television. They added perhaps a cruise round the British Isles where they could stop off to see places like Edinburgh, Dublin, Liverpool and so on could be arranged after the wedding. They also asked us the feasibility of popping over to Paris, Amsterdam and Monte Carlo.

Money seemed no object. Rishi's father owned a factory which had imported and exported spices and since the rise of popularity in Indian food the business had done particularly well over the last twenty or so years.

His mother, being a bit of a social climber, also wanted a grand Jaipur wedding for us. They had a large circle of friends and business colleagues who I guessed she wanted to impress. "Oh Leah, You will make such a beautiful Jaipur bride. We will have a traditional wedding with all the special touches. Just say what you want when you and Rishi have discussed it and we will arrange and pay for everything. 'Wow. That is generous' I thought.

It was all possible. So with these exciting thoughts rushing round our heads we saw his parents and Archan off in their taxi .
The remaining days were spent doing lots of sightseeing and booked excursions. We had a wonderful time but it went so fast. There was a lot to see and do but we saved some highlights for another time.
Guy and Monica continued to be good company in the evenings at the hotel. Tired after our days out we enjoyed a few relaxing drinks, Scrabble and card games. We exchanged addresses and promised to tell them the date of our weddings. "We want to raise a glass or two on the big day. We could even turn up if invited."

Rishi's father offered to take us back to the airport for our return to London in his chauffeur driven car. We gratefully accepted. His mother came too.

On the journey they spoke about how heartbroken they had been, how they were pleased that the family rift had been mended and how they could see that Rishi had chosen a perfect match.

'Phew, 'I thought. 'This could have all gone wrong.'

The subject of our second ceremony in India came up again. " Don't forget. We want you to discuss and decide what you want your Indian wedding to include. As we have said before, it will be our joy and privilege to arrange a huge celebration with everything you want. Please, just let us know and give us enough time to arrange things."

"Thank you, and yes, we will." Rishi said. "That is really generous of you." "Thank you." I whispered, bowled over by their generousity.

The airport came in sight. Time to say goodbye. His mother, Sharmila, fell into Rishi's arms and tears rolled down her cheeks. "My son, my son," she cried. "Your mother's love is with you always.""The miles cannot break our family bond. It is far too strong" said Pradeep as he waved goodbye to us at the airport, a tear in his eye.
So back home after a wonderful and fruitful visit. We had everything to look forward to.

CHAPTER 34

Back to normality

We were soon both immersed in the everyday dramas and routines of our jobs. The working weeks ticked by in normality.

Our first plan of action for the Indian side of the celebrations was to tell Rishi's parents what we had decided. Our Civil ceremony would take place in England with Rishi's family attending followed shortly after by an Indian wedding in Rishi's home town, Jaipur.

We wanted his parents to choose the guest list as only my mother and I would be coming from England. We knew that they had friends, relations and business people who they wanted to invite and as they were hosting the event they could have as many guests as they wanted.

We wanted our wedding to be traditionally Indian so that Mum and I could have an interesting experience. That was all we stipulated as we asked for the rest to be a surprise for both of us.

"Don't tell us" Rishi pleaded ."We will love whatever you put on for us. We are very excited."

That is how we left things-in their hands. Generously Rishi would pay Mum's and my fare out to India.

We booked the flights for July as soon as the dates were decided, so as to keep the cost down. For Mum it would be am absolutely marvellous experience as she hadn't been so far a field before.

Rishi had been property hunting for our first home but wasn't having much luck. Property in London was very expensive and you didn't get much for your money.

I had heard from Mum. Apparently Phil had been accepted for a Masters Degree course at the University of Lancashire.

He had stayed at her house while going through the interview process. He would begin in October.

I was pleased that Phil had got his Uni place as he was a good deserving man. Mum told me that in the cut-throat music industry he had found it hard to get promotion. Maybe his Masters Degree would open a few doors for him.

Rishi and I arranged a whistle-stop tour to see Mum and book our wedding at the seafront registry office in Blackpool, the modern Wedding Chapel.

It was an unusual but exciting place to have our civil ceremony and pertinent to my past life and the love I have for my home town.

We needed to book a confirmed date so that Rishi's family could arrange flights and all the other things on their agenda.

For them it was a trip of a lifetime and we wanted to help make it special. We arranged for the Blackpool wedding to take place on a Friday, in June the following year.
The weather should be reasonable, not too hot, long light evenings and it fitted in with a lovely cruise around the United Kingdom for his parents to go onto afterwards.

We booked them into a five star hotel ninety miles away in the Lake District. We wanted them to experience England at its best and most beautiful and that seemed the ideal place.

Rishi and I had been accepted for a mortgage but couldn't find anything that suited us. We had our priority list. Near to work, small garden, not too much to do to make it nice and of course a ceiling price. This was our criteria.

We were let down a couple of times at the early stages when we got in a chain of buyers and due to the chain our chosen house went to someone else.

That was disappointing as I had already got far too excited and had selected furniture and had decor in my mind.

'Don't fall into that trap again' I told myself. Yet one day I found the most perfect little house. It hardly needed any work and was only six years old. It was one of four starter homes built on the plot of one now demolished old house.
"We are so lucky. I can even walk to work from here" I told Mum. I had set my heart on it, despite trying hard not to put myself in that position but I just couldn't help it.The excitement had got to me. We had a survey done earlier which cost us quite a bit and then just before getting to the contract stage I got a 'phone call from the estate agent.

"Your buyer has unfortunately taken his house off the market" said a woman on the other end of the 'phone. I was told this shattering news in such a matter of fact way, as if it was nothing.

"But we have paid for a survey and were ready to sign." I replied. "Yes Madam, but the contract has not been signed. Do accept our apologies" said the uncaring voice.I felt absolutely devastated.

That evening, when Rishi and I discussed what had happened he said. "You know what Leah, I have had enough of this. We have scrimped and saved for a tiny house. You have been let down by estate agents and sellers alike. I'm just not having this"

Then Rishi announced totally out of the blue." For the kind of money they want in London and what you get for your pounds why don't we go and live in the north. How would you feel about a little house in the countryside maybe nearer your Mum? I know that you love Lancashire. To be honest I could do with moving jobs and having a change."
This tack took me completely by surprise but I didn't need much persuading. "OK, get the job first and then we can weigh it all up." I said.

That evening I told my housemate Jessica, whose view I respected. She thought Rishi had the right idea. "Its not like you haven't tried to buy in London Leah" she said. "You have been so let down." Ellen commented that if she settled down with her current doctor boyfriend it wouldn't be in London. Jasmine said "I think London can be a tough place to live. What if you have a family. Wouldn't the countryside be a better place for them to grow up in?" Mary, the last to join our house said that we should think carefully as there were more job opportunities in London. The housemates had all made sensible and valid points. After much soul searching, Rishi and I decided to give Lancashire a try.

During the next three months Rishi applied for posts out of London. He had some interviews but the competition was hard. He suspected someone younger and therefore cheaper always got the job. Eventually his luck changed. He was, at last, called for an interview as a Prescribing Practice Pharmacist, working alongside medical staff at a large Doctor's practice.
"Leah." he said. "Let's go through these requirements. Can I meet the criteria? Poor Rishi had got to the stage when he even doubted his own ability. He read the job description.

'Medication queries and signing medicines. Reconciliation face to face and telephone medication Reviews and call backs. Management of chronic diseases. Support and develop safe prescribing procedures Work alongside nurses, GP's and other health care professionals. Reviewing Quality and Outcomes Framework. To identify Patient's in need of intervention and attend Practice and Network meetings.'
"Well, yes, you can do most of that. I don't think that you have much experience of the Quality and Outcomes Framework. Isn't that to do with meeting standards in GP's surgeries?" I asked. "You are right, yes and I'm sure I could learn about that easily." said Rishi sounding quite keen. With that he completed the online application form and sent it through email. "In for a

penny, in for a pound" he said.

Six weeks later Rishi had a successful interview and took the post. It was agreed that he could take leave to go to India for our Indian wedding ceremony. What could be better, our future was in the pot.

Soon after Rishi left London and went to live in a studio flat near Mum. It worked out quite nicely as Rishi got to know Mum better, was on hand for any wedding decisions and financially was good for Rishi.

We had a mortgage and perhaps a house on the horizon so any way of saving a bit for legal fees was a bonus. He had a comfortable base until he had found a home for both of us. I missed him terribly. We spoke and Skyped frequently but of course it wasn't like having the love of your life by your side.

Rishi enjoyed his new position at the Doctor's practice. It was always busy he told me but more friendly and personal as the patients were often regulars coming in for prescriptions. "Northerners are very friendly" he told me over the 'phone. He had a bit more opportunity to pass the time of day with the patients too.
In London it had been rush, rush, rush and he'd never see that person again. Here, in Lancashire, he had made friends with one of the Doctors and they had gone out walking a couple of times at the weekend.

Rishi had also got into running and a few of the Practice staff had gone on lunchtime runs together with stopwatches, trying to better their performances and fitness levels. I felt relieved that he had found this new lifestyle to be compatible with his new circumstances. Life was good.

Rishi travelled by car to the new job in Skemersdale just outside Liverpool. It took him less than an hour to get there. The traffic wasn't like London, stop, start. Here he kept moving. He told me it was fine as he had the radio on and he quite enjoyed the journey.

Meanwhile, in London I began to scour the Internet to find a wedding dress. I went to a couple of wedding shops with Jessica. She had an eye for fashion and gave her usual good advice. I tried a few traditional gowns but felt they were a bit over the top. "Oh no Leah. It's just not you. It's not a good shape on you and doesn't fit your personality." said Jessica. What's more she was absolutely right. I couldn't find anything that I was happy with so I decided to save my money and settled for a less expensive but still beautiful cream lace off the peg midi length dress. It flattered my figure and looked expensive. I also felt that it was more suitable for a registry office wedding. I knew that once in India I would be getting the full works.

I went up to Blackpool to spend some time with Mum and Rishi to make the final preparations.
Rishi needed kitting out for the occasion. All that hill running had given him an athletic build, even a six pack. He would look wonderful in his wedding suit. He opted for a three piece lounge suit made to measure in a lightweight pale blue fabric to give a bit of style to the romance of the occasion. It would be something a bit different.

We ordered some quite extravagant flowers. A red rose bouquet for me and red corsages for the mothers, not forgetting button holes for the men. I thought red appropriate as it is the traditional colour for weddings in India. In addition we ordered a small red rose arrangement for the top of our wedding cake and a few loose extra small roses of the same kind to go around the cake. I was planning to save a bit of money on the cake. I planned buy some ready iced tiers and assemble it myself.

My faithful old friend from school, Lynne was to be my bridesmaid. "Oh Leah. Are you sure? Thank you for asking me." She sounded thrilled." Lynne, you have helped me get over bad times in my life. You are a true friend." I said.

The two of us went to Manchester for the best choice of bridesmaid dresses. We found a stunning midi dress with a tulip skirt in the same cream as my lace dress but with a wide pale blue sash the shade of Rishi's suit. "It's perfect." I gushed. The blue covered buttons down the back completed the look and it fitted Lynne like a glove. She looked lovely.

We visited some wedding venues and settled for a swanky hotel in upmarket Lytham St Anne's, not too far from Blackpool. It had a feel of luxury about it with rich soft furnishings, silky cushions and light furniture.I knew it would please Rishi's mother and look good in any photographs. His mother would be able to show all her friends with pride. Another benefit was that Rishi's parents could spend a couple of days here before the wedding as well as being on site for the reception.

Lytham St Anne's had lots of little individual shops and there were plenty of little tea shops too. All giving a very impressive English experience.

Cars and a photographer that Mum knew of were booked for the big day and with that all we had to do was wait until June.

CHAPTER 35

A house of our own

There was a lot of decisions to be made about where we should live. Over the phone, while Rishi was in Lancashire and me in London, we discussed it relentlessly.

We made a list of all the things that were important to us. It grew longer and longer. "We are not going to get everything. It's impossible. I said. "Well, lets write them down and then at least we have a starting point for everything we wanted" Rishi suggested." Ok, here goes, detached, garden, three bedrooms, new or nearly new, garage, shed, large kitchen, utility room, downstairs loo" he said. "OK, not too far from Mum, near the hospital for my work if I can get a job there. I need to be near shops, bus routes and a main town with at least one department store plus all the usual stores and near a station" I suggested. "Near a pub more likely" said Rishi. We laughed.

It was exciting to wish and hope for all of these things but we had a financial ceiling and knew that everything was not possible. We were both realistic down to earth people and realised that half of our wish list was out of the question.

We searched the Internet, It was hard being apart but necessary. If things go our way we will have a new home to live in after our wedding in Blackpool and failing that after we had been to India.

I made plans to go up for a whistle-stop tour so Rishi and I could go house hunting. We decided to try to settle near the University town of Preston. It is a lovely historic town and would be quite close to Mum, and to Lynne, my best friend. I knew quite a few people in the area. I liked the town centre. It has lots of nice shops, a huge historic open market and the countryside would be close. It is about 15 miles from the coast of Blackpool and the M6 was very close for Rishi to get to work.

It was great to see Rishi in the flesh again. I had got up early that morning and made a special effort in clothes, hair and make up. I knew I looked good. It was a pity that it was a damp and rainy morning in London, the kind of day that gets into your bones and ruins your hair. I caught the train to Preston where Rishi picked me up. I was so excited to see him again. We ran into each others arms outside the station and then just sat in the car and just kissed and cuddled for the next five minutes. True love is a wonderful feeling.

We drove off to a residential area just on the outskirts of Preston. We had pinpointed it as a possible place to live.
"I have a big surprise for you." Rishi said in an excited voice. "My parents are giving us some money to help us to get our first house. We have been given fifty thousand pounds, or there about, depending on the exchange rate from rupees." My heart missed as beat.
"Fifty thousand pounds? Really? That's huge." It took me a while to digest this news due to the shock. "Wow, we can now look at better houses. We might even be able to get most of our wish list. I can't believe it. I really just can't believe it. That is so good of your parents," I said excitedly.

We parked the car and had a wander round to get an updated feel of the area. It was not disappointing, in fact quite the opposite. It felt like an area that had a bright future. There were a lot of young people about the streets and plenty of building developments going on.

"Come on Leah. Lets go for a drink and mull the outskirts of Preston over before our appointment with the estate agent. He

has sorted out three new builds for us to view." So we wandered down the road and soon came to a pub where we found a quiet corner and resumed our catch up session .We looked excitedly on Rishi's laptop at houses close by that were for sale. "It's a big decision." Rishi said wisely. "Don't let us make a mistake. It's our future. We mustn't settle for less than our dream home."
At three in the afternoon we met the estate agent and he took us in his car to a brand new development five miles from Preston. It was on a bus route and not too far from a train station. Perfect I thought. Time was of the essence as I had to be back in London for my late shift the following afternoon so we had to make a decision if any of these homes fitted the bill.

I had driven myself insane looking at different houses on the Internet and ruling them out one by one. Too expensive, too near a main road, no bus route nearby, too far to walk to the shops and so on. It was a minefield. I had lived in the area until making my move to London so knew it well.

Mum came along to lend her support. We viewed the show house which was furnished with up to the minute furniture and fittings. It had the wow factor. "The garage is a double" said Rishi excitedly. I stood in the house and asked myself "Could I live here?" The answer was a huge YES. Of the three houses that we viewed the layout was better in the show house as the ground floor was bigger and the sitting room had a triple aspect with a view of open fields. "This is the one," I shouted excitedly and ran over to hug Rishi. "Love it" said Mum. "I can get here on the bus easily from Blackpool too, that's if I don't want to take the car out."

With that we went back to the office to sort out the paperwork in euphoric moods. We were both so excited. The move up north had been the right decision. Rishi Skyped his parents to tell them our good news. He sent a short video of the house for them to see too. The wonders of technology. We said a huge 'Thank you' to Rishi's parents for their generosity. This was more than I ever expected.

CHAPTER 36

The Wedding

What began as a small wedding seemed to grow and grow. It was important to Mum that our relatives should be invited as I was her only child so there wouldn't be anymore weddings. We sent out pretty printed invitations to invite friends and our small family. "Mustn't forget Auntie Daphne. Haven't seen her for quite some time" said Mum, "and cousin Joan. They will be thrilled to come."

We even invited Guy and Monica from New York, the people that we had met in India. We had kept in touch with them regularly through the email It was a shock when they replied that they were coming to 'do the UK' and incorporate our wedding. We were delighted. "They are such fun people that they will keep things going "said Rishi. Rishi got in touch with them to see if there was any advice he could give about what to do, where to stay and what to see. It seemed that they had done their research and had booked a week in London staying at the Waldorf Hotel. They were to go to The National Gallery, Walton's Music Hall, The Victoria and Albert Museum and the South Bank Festival Halls. They had tickets for a river trip to Hampton Court, Ladies Day at Sandown Park race course, Windsor Castle and motor racing at Brands Hatch. Then they had plans to go to Cornwall staying at Port Isaac, Wales to see Snowdon and finally Edinburgh. Wow, what an itinerary. Our wedding would come somewhere in the middle. It would be lovely to see them again if they hadn't worn themselves out as tourists!

Time passed quickly with the new house and wedding plans keeping us busy. We signed up for the house without a hitch and Rishi moved into our brand new Preston house. "I love it here Leah. It is such a peaceful spot." Between us and the computer we chose enough furniture to start our new life, keeping things to a minimum until we got the feel of the place.

The next big thing for me was to get another job so I applied to the Royal Preston Hospital as it was nearest. I was called up for an interview and was immediately offered a post in the Orthopaedic Department. "Lady Luck is on my side" I said "Told you" said my friend Lynne.

That night Rishi and I went for a celebration candle-lit meal in a little French restaurant near one of the beautiful Lancashire villages. Once seated Rishi fumbled in his pocket and brought out an expensive looking box. "Leah, I want you to accept this necklace and bracelet as a token of my love and admiration for you. It will match your engagement ring and I hope that you will wear these at our wedding." Fumbling awkwardly I opened the gift box and there were two stunning pieces of jewellery made of gold and diamonds. I really felt that I didn't deserve such an expensive and unexpected gift. "These are gifts from my family" said Rishi. I was almost speechless. I hadn't expected anything, let alone two precious pieces of jewellery. "I love them both. They are absolutely beautiful. Thank you." I could hardly say the words. I put my hand in his and gave it an extra hard squeeze. It seemed that we were so lucky. I felt blessed. Everything was falling into place.

The wedding month of June finally arrived. Such a lovely month. Rishi's parents travelled from India for our wedding. They touched down at Manchester Airport and Rishi met them, taking them straight to their hotel in the beautiful Lake District. They were exhausted after their long journey. Apparently they had a baby crying all night on the flight so they didn't get any sleep. Rishi spent the next two days at the hotel to settle them in and to catch up on all their news. He managed to take them out and about, visiting the little villages and lakes, sampling the local hospitality. They both fell in love with the beautiful area.

Four days before the wedding I left work. It was an emotional parting as we had got fond of each other. I had loved my time in London and felt grateful for everything that it had given me. The team had generously bought me a gift voucher so that I could buy something for the home. "That way you don't have to carry heavy gifts up to Preston." they said.

I had been very happy at the hospital and lucky enough to have things work out so well for me. I had to give a little 'Thank you' speech when I reminisced about a couple of funny incidents that we had shared which would always remain with me. I got really choked up and the tears flowed. Quite unusual for me as I always considered myself to be a toughie. It was an emotional time and a big step.

I packed up belongings in the house and gave my room a spring clean for the next occupier. That evening I took the girls from the house out for a small hen night. We started out in the Italian restaurant and ended up in a cocktail bar celebrating with an excess of alcohol. We exchanged lots of promises to keep in touch. They had been such supportive colleagues and I appreciated their friendship.

Next morning with a bit of a hangover, a large suitcase and heavy holdall I set off for Preston and a new life. It was the morning after the night before and I took the opportunity to sleep for most of the journey to recover. Rishi met me at the station with a beautiful bunch of red roses, just like the ones we had ordered for our wedding. "Well, it's finally going to happen Leah. I just can't wait until Friday."

We went straight to our new house and he picked me up in his strong manly arms and carried me over the threshold. "We have to do these traditional things" he said laughing.

It was wonderful to see Rishi again and this time it was for good. I wouldn't be leaving for London again.

Early that evening I went to stay at Mum's. I wanted to get

married from Mum's where my childhood memories rested. I needed to reminisce about my past and have peace and time to think about my Dad. For the next two days I soaked up the homely atmosphere, Mum treated me like a Princess and fussed about me. Sadly, Dad was there only in spirit, not to give me away, so thinking about him and the happy times was the best I could do, the nearest that I could get to him.

While at Mum's I used the spare bedroom. I went to put my underwear in the drawer and was rather surprised to find some men's clothing neatly stacked in the drawers. This was not the time to bring it up so I put it to the back of my mind. There was probably a simple explanation. Maybe they had been left by Rishi when he came to live close by.

The day of the wedding arrived. There was a ring at the doorbell. Mum had organised a make-up artist and the hairdresser as a lovely surprise to make us all look beautiful for the midday wedding. I wasn't having a veil or hat. Instead I had chosen an ornate and intricate net and jewelled hair comb which would catch the light and sparkle. It was quite a showstopper that was worn at a jaunty angle. Blackpool was a great place to purchase blingy sparkly items.It was itself a blingy, sparkly place.

The doorbell rang and my bouquet arrived. It was beautiful, as was Mum's corsage and Lynne's posy. Just as I wanted. We put on our dresses. I was thrilled with mine and felt that I had got it just right for a Registry Office wedding. Lynne looked perfect. Mum, looking slim and beautiful, every bit the Mother of the Bride, wearing a silver grey coloured lace dress and satin jacket and a large stylish hat. She carried a silk clutch bag with matching shoes. On my feet were a very high glamorous cream pair of heels. I just hoped these are going to be comfortable. We looked and felt fabulous, the absolute business and were so excited.

Mum cracked open a bottle of cold champagne, we toasted ourselves then had a second glass for Dutch courage. Finally I put on the beautiful jewellery, a bracelet and necklace that Rishi had given me as a wedding gift from his family.

On the way to the Registry Office I thanked Mum for my happy childhood, her love, support and advice. Without Mum's encouragement after the break-up with Dan I wouldn't have gone to London and be where I am today. So I told her.

We all got into the wedding cars and glided off effortlessly to the Wedding Chapel, a strange shaped building set right on the promenade. Rishi was waiting outside with his brother Archan, who had arrived only yesterday, to take on the role of Best Man. Rishi spotted the car. His face lit up and he entered the building to take his place for the ceremony. I gave Mum a big hug.

As I walked in on Mum's arm I could see all eyes were on us. It felt quite emotional and I was a bit shaky. My bouquet was even quivering, yet at the same time I felt confident that I was doing the right thing by marrying Rishi. "Here goes" I said, as I made my way towards Rishi. I felt that I was going to burst with happiness. Rishi looked stunning in his suit and crisp white shirt. Our eyes met and we both had the biggest smile ever.
I caught a glimpse of Rishi's mother who looked like she approved. Thank goodness for that. I could see that she was taking it all in and no doubt it would be relayed in great detail to her circle of wealthy friends in Jaipur. His father stood upright, looking proud of his first born son.

I got through the ceremony remembering to speak up so everyone could hear the vows. Rishi too spoke with confidence, seemingly unperturbed by the occasion. His private education had given him a lot of confidence. The Registrar led us through the procedure to the end when she announced " You are now husband and wife. You may kiss your bride" Rishi turned to me and we kissed. " The new Mrs. Jain " he whispered in my ear. The guests cheered and clapped noisily. I looked into Rishi's big brown eyes and knew that we were the perfect match, the best forever friends.

CHAPTER 37

The Reception

We arrived at the hotel and were greeted with a welcome glass of champagne.

Jean, a friend of Mum's was doing the photography so we posed for the usual and a few not so usual shots.   We had requested that some of the photos be natural shots rather than lots of people standing still posin.

Our guests began to arrive and we formed a chain at the door to greet them. It was just as I wanted. Informal, friendly and classy.
The guests, all looking fabulous mingled, chatted and weemed to approve. I spotted Aunt Daphne in a well matched hat and dress and cousin Joan in a blue midi outfit, as usual carrying far too much in her big bag. However it was Sharmila, Rishi's mother who stole the show. She was dressed in a breathtaking traditional purple and red silk sari with lavish embroidery in gold threads and beads. His father, Pradeep, wore the traditional made to measure kurta in rich red silk and tightly fitting churidas. On his head was a red silk turban. He could have been a Maharaja himself.
The cake looked the part on its three tiered stand with the fresh rosebuds on top, with more around the base of each tier.
Fiona, the daughter of another of Mum's friends played some romantic, classy tunes on her clarinet as background music.

We took our places at the table and the meal was delicious, three courses served in style by a team of well trained eastern European staff.
It was then I noticed that Monica and Guy were missing. Their places at the table were empty. I whispered to Rishi. Why they were missing was a mystery. Rishi last heard from Guy when he rang saying that they had arrived safely, had a great time in Lon-

don and were going down to Cornwall for the next part of their holiday.

Archan and Lynne sat next to each other and seemed deeply engrossed in conversation. My Aunt Lucy had met up with her cousin George from my fathers side. Shrieks of laughter came from their table as he told one of the exaggerated stories that he was famous for. "George is off" whispered Mum to me.

Mum bravely got up to thank everyone for coming but just that moment the doors opened and I glimpsed Guy and Monica coming through the shiny double door. Nothing Guy ever did was subtle. He made a noisy entrance as he called across the table to Rishi. "Sorry we missed the service. Got held up with a flight to Manchester. Couldn't drive here as I have broken my leg."

"It could only happen to you Guy" said. Rishi, pleased that they had made it.

Rishi asked the staff to get them both a meal and fill their glasses. It seemed that Guy had been on the beach enjoying the seaside experience in north Cornwall. They were walking on the rocks, looking out for crabs in the rock pools when Guy had slipped on a slimy rock and landed heavily on his leg breaking it. It gave everyone nearby a good laugh and Guy held his crutch in the air and waved it almost in victory.

Mum did really well with her speech. She reflected on how she had been left widowed by her dear husband having to bring me up as a single parent. I was pleased that she had mentioned Dad, so he was included. Mum continued. How proud she was that I had achieved so much. Mum welcomed Rishi into our family and thanked everyone for coming, especially Sharmila and Pradeep, Monica and Guy, all who had made long journeys. It was the perfect speech, not too long and expressing all the important things. She finished off with a perfect piece of poetry that she said summed up the love she sees between Rishi and me. I have to admit the poem brought tears to my eyes. I felt really proud of my Mum.

We hadn't wanted an evening reception so after the meal and speeches we went to another plush room with lots of deep soft sofas. Everyone got time to mingle and chat. We had hired a talented young musician from the Royal Northern College of Music to play the sitar to add a touch of India. It was a lovely sound and was just perfect for the occasion. The instrument rang out creating a warm and happy atmosphere. A little touch of Rishi's home country to help Sharmila and Pradeep feel at ease. The bar was open so everyone topped up their glasses. Mum and Sharmila chatted like they had known each other for years. Guy was on spirits so was soon performing in his gregarious style despite the crutches. Monica, by his side, still with her huge red fingernails looking lovingly in admiration, as he held an audience.

Before the wedding party disbanded tea was served together with some small Indian sweets made from almonds and sugar. We had discovered these delicacies at a speciality shop and placed an order when out in one day in Manchester. It was the perfect touch for a perfect wedding.

We took a taxi back to home, laden with lovely presents, wedding cake and flowers.

We just collapsed on the new sofas and chilled out exhausted.

CHAPTER 38

And so to my new home

"Well Mrs. Jain. How do you feel the wedding went? Were you pleased with everything?" said Rishi, in the morning as he opened his eyes. "I loved every minute. I'm really glad that I came back to Mum's house. That was so important to me. I had that few days to reminisce about my childhood and my father which I hadn't been able to do when in London."

"Yes, time to think is important especially about your father " he said understandingly.

We chatted generally about the wedding. "What did you think then Rishi?" I asked. "Loved it. You looked so beautiful Leah" "Aww. Thanks" I said. "I was really pleased with the choices we made for the reception. That worked very well. A good mix of different music from both cultures too. Your parents seemed to enjoy it. I'm pleased that they mixed in so well as I wasn't sure that they would, being that it is so different over here. It must have been an interesting experience for them."
"Yes, that is what they said to me" replied Rishi" "But I think that I need to check that everything is well with them. My mother would expect me to. They have another three days at the hotel before joining the ship for their cruise, so we need to spend a bit of time with them. I said I'd take them to Liverpool Docks to pick up their ship." "That's fine by me. It will make life easier for them."

I felt that we had to do everything we could to ensure they enjoyed their time here. "We will be able to see more of them when we fly out for our second wedding."

"Can't wait." said Rishi.

Rishi had an idea. "Let's invite them to see our house tomorrow, say late afternoon. It will give us time to get some nice food in. Let us ask Archan, Lynne and your mother too. I have had this idea in my mind for a while but didn't say anything in case it was all too much."

"OK, Great." I said, reaching for the mobile and making the necessary calls. It was going to be another party.

"Why don't we ask Guy and Monica to come, especially as they are booked into my parents hotel. I can pick them all up in the people carrier. It can be a housewarming too."

So the plans were made. It was a busy morning with the mobiles going off, Mum calling to say she would pick up Lynne tomorrow. Guy and Monica replying to our text message. Archan wanting to speak to his brother, his parents checking what time they had to be ready and the hotel saying that someone had left a silk stole at the reception.
So today, our first day as a married couple, in our spanking new home, was a busy one. We had to buy some extra china as we only had the bare minimum of plates and pudding bowls in the house. We stopped in the shop while we went through a mental checklist to make sure we could put a dinner on a plate and a pudding in a bowl.

Home we went, laughing about how it would look to Rishi's mother if we hadn't got enough china and couldn't serve a guest dinner. "She would be mortified" he said laughing.

At four o'clock the following day our guests arrived. We had put some of our new garden furniture out so that our guests could enjoy the lovely June sunshine.

We were lucky to have a south-facing garden which caught the sun all afternoon. It was a perfect summer's day with a light breeze. We had made an elderflower punch and had plenty of wine to offer the guests, so soon our back garden was buzzing with chatter.

Rishi's mother and father sat under the sun-shade. They said that they saw enough of the sun at home.

Lynne, my bridesmaid and Archan took themselves off to a corner where I had put some large soft Indian floor cushions to sit on. They chatted away happily.

Guy and Monica sat next to Rishi's parents. Guy with his plastered leg on the footstool. Pradeep and Guy seemed to really hit it off. Both had experienced interesting lives, had achieved a lot and talked continuously about politics and business. Guy cracking the jokes and Pradeep roaring and shaking with laughter.

I was so pleased that our invitation had extended to Guy and Monica. She was more than happy to soak up the late afternoon sun and chill out with her long fingers wrapped around a glass of wine.

Rishi kept the conversation going and the drinks flowing. He was good at that sort of thing. His customer care training at work plus his private education had given him just the right experience.

Mum helped me prepare the meal in the kitchen. Unexpectedly her mobile phone rang. "Oh, hello darling" she said. Yes, it was wonderful. It all went smoothly. I'm at Leah's at the moment. Can't really talk now. Lots to tell you. Speak properly tomorrow, at home. Love you. Bye."

I could hear that it was a man's voice. Mum didn't know that I had overheard the conversation. That's a bit mysterious I thought. Who was she speaking to?

It wasn't the time to pry so I just got on with things.

Rishi did a grand tour of the house. His mother loved it and eagerly took photos on her phone to impress her friends. "We only have it half furnished. When it's finished it will look even more fantastic. It's thanks to you for the financial help that we find ourselves in this lovely house." he said discretely to his father.

We had decided to keep the food simple but traditional giving our guests a taste of English cuisine. We went for a roast chicken dinner with accompaniments. It was something that I felt confident to cook as I had done this many times at home with Mum. As a new housewife I wasn't used to cooking for larger numbers so we bought chicken breasts. "Great portion control" said Rishi.

I had laid the table indoors with the help of a wooden sheet that went on top of our small table, so extending it.

Mum had brought some fold up chairs from home, so we were all set. We sat round and fortunately, mainly due to luck, I served up the best meal that I had ever cooked. Everything was good. Crispy potatoes, stuffing balls, gravy with no lumps and three kinds of fresh vegetable! "This is great. A true English roast." said Guy, still with his leg on the footstool. "You have a wife who can cook Rishi. Why can't you cook a meal like this Monica"? he joked.

The dessert came next, an English trifle made with sponge cakes and custard. It got a great response. I beamed.

Rishi's Mum and my Mum both had a good sense of humour. They told after dinner stories about when we were little children and some of the sweet things we had done. "When he was only four years old Rishi had slipped out of the flat and picked some flowers from the garden below. He then tried to sell them to anyone passing. His Nanny hadn't noticed he'd gone. I was panic stricken but when I found him he had a pocket full of rupees. I was furious. We sacked his Nanny"

That caused a laugh. Mum responded with her own little funny story about me. Rishi and I exchanged glances and a giggle.

I wondered if we would ever have a family and have funny little tales to relate.

"Where have the years gone?" said Mum." I really don't know" said Sharmila. "It has gone so fast, just slipped by."

The evening was warm and balmy and after the meal we went back into the garden until it got dark. We lit lots of garden candles which added to the ambiance. Lynne helped me make a hot drink for everyone before going home. She whispered to me that she would be seeing Archan tomorrow for a date. I was glad that my wedding had introduced these two well matched young people to each other. Who knows where it may go.

So my first bash at entertaining had been a hit. Sharmila kissed me goodbye and thanked me." Leah. You are going to make Rishi a lovely wife and I will see you in Jaipur in July. Trust me, it will all be a lovely surprise."

Rishi drove the guests home. Guy, the worst for drink, and singing at the top of his voice, while brandishing his crutch out of the car window. The car disappeared out of sight.......

CHAPTER 39

We arrive in India

We had a call from Rishi's parents to say that, following our wedding, they had enjoyed their cruise round the British Isles, had met lots of interesting people, made new friends and seen some wonderful places. Their suite was delightful and the service excellent.

"Glad it worked well for them. Cruising can be relaxing after a busy wedding plus England looks great at this time of year" said Rishi.

They had followed up the cruise with a visit to Paris on Eurostar, then by a flight for a three-day break in Amsterdam. They had enjoyed both capital cities especially the Amsterdam Rijks Museum. "The artworks were amazing. Such treasures" said Sharmila.

Now settled home, back in Jaipur, Sharmila and Pradeep had been a having a busy time arranging things for our second traditionally Indian wedding.

They had, apparently, enjoyed the planning and were excited about the arrangements that they had made for us.

There were only a few last minute things they still had to do. Things that had to be done on our big day.

Pradeep had earlier booked us all into the four star Chomu Palace Hotel for a week. One day was to recover from our journey, one day to meet up with his parents then one day was set aside for the wedding service and reception with two days set aside for relaxation.

Pradeep had even arranged some sightseeing for Mum as it was her first time in India. A family meal had been planned for another day and the final day was allocated as time to get packed up, say our goodbye's and return home.

It was certainly going to be an action packed week. Rishi's parents appreciated that our time was short as we both had limited leave and had to get back to work.

I looked the hotel up on the Internet. Wow. It was amazing. Opulent with exquisite architecture, big open courtyards with palm trees and filigree arches. There was an outdoor swimming pool, a health spa with a plethora of treatments and a gym. The hotel was surrounded by beautiful manicured flower beds and grass areas to relax in with sumptuous garden furniture. I didn't say anything to Rishi. It would be a nice surprise for him.

The flight went smoothly. We touched down at Delhi Airport and waited for our connecting flight to Jaipur.
Rishi sent his mother a text. It was too early in the morning to speak. She would still be asleep.
'Arrived safely. Now at Delhi. Looking forward to seeing you to-morrow. Need to sleep. Leah and Rishi XX'
We finally touched down in Jaipur where a taxi was waiting to take us to the hotel. Exhausted, we fell into an amazing four poster bed after a quick wash and brush-up.

We were too exhausted to appreciate our surroundings at that point. Amazingly Mum had weathered the journey better than us. Her adrenalin was on a high. She went to her luxurious room but later told us she had been too excited to sleep.

We met up later in the plush restaurant of the Chomu Palace. We ordered afternoon tea, now somewhat recovered from our long journey. Looking round we could appreciate the lavishness of this hotel. It did not disappoint. The beautiful ornate inter-ior, the chandeliers and the extravagant soft furnishings. A great place for our wedding.
But an early night for all was on the cards as tomorrow we were to meet up with Rishi's parents and there was plenty to do with just the one day before the wedding.

It was muggy the next day when we took a taxi to Sharmila and Pradeep's central Jaipur flat.

We were greeted warmly. "I'm so excited" I told Sharmila as we held hands and hugged. Rishi shook his fathers hand and Mum, finding the heat and closeness exhausting, found a chair to collapse into. It was 30 degrees, cloudy and stuffy with Jaipur dust and pollution evident.
Fortunately Pradeep had arranged for all of us to spend a relaxing day at their hill-station out of town. The chauffeur was summoned. With relief we ascended to a higher altitude bringing respite from the close atmosphere.

"July is a monsoon month so we could expect rain tomorrow. It's not an ideal month for a wedding but fingers crossed" said Sharmila in a worried tone. "On the bright side it is early in July, so fortunately the chances of rain are less."
I had already discovered that it wasn't the best time of year for a wedding in India but the wedding had to fit in with our work schedule.
"We have arranged for the majority of the wedding to take place inside the Chomu Palace Hotel. Can't have our beautiful bride getting caught in monsoon rain" said Pradeep.
We were reassured that there was good air conditioning in all the rooms where the festivities were to take place, so the guests should be comfortable.

The day passed by congenially. We ate, drank, told his parents about our new jobs and the things that we had bought for our new house.

Rishi and his father discussed who would be coming to the celebration. "There were to be lots of cousins, aunts and uncles, a few of your old friends, my business colleagues with their families, your mother and my friends and acquaintances, a total of almost two hundred people." advised Pradeep. "It's a small wedding" said Sharmila. "Well that is by Indian standards."

I gasped.

While at the hill station Rishi's mother told me that she had my wedding dress and it was laid out in one of the bedrooms ready for me to try on.

I was familiar with Indian gowns having researched them online. All Indian gowns are beautiful and Sharmila had very good taste so I wasn't worried.

I had given my measurements to her when in Blackpool. "Close your eyes Leah" Sharmila said as she led me towards the bedroom excited to show me.

"You can open them now" she said excitedly.

There, laid out, was the most stunning Indian wedding dress. I was blown away. "Oh. It looks beautiful." And it was. Sharmila told me she had chosen a modern version of a traditional Indian dress and incorporated some elements of western style. "I knew that you'd feel more comfortable in that." I agreed. There was the basic red dress which was cut so there was a seam under the bust. Round the neck were traditional Indian patterns embroidered in gold thread with hundreds of tiny gold beads. The skirt went to mid length and had a shaped hem falling lower at the back than the front, a fashionable touch seen in England. Underneath this midi skirt was another full length skirt which was so heavily embroidered that it looked like a band of gold. A huge embellished red, pink and cream scarf which toned, complementing the dress, was to be worn like a shawl. It was all amazing.

"It's not too heavy" said Sharmila. "Some of the gowns are uncomfortable to wear. I think you will get on well with this. Try it on but Rishi mustn't see you in it.

It's a surprise. Rishi's red turban will complement your shawl as it is the same colour." I tried the dress on and had that moment when I couldn't believe how I looked. Never in my wildest dreams had I ever envisaged wearing a full Indian costume and getting married in India.

It is every girls dream to look good in bridal attire and I knew my dream would be fulfilled.

"There were some accessories to wear too." nodded Sharmila. A headdress with an jewel embossed circle that would sit on my forehead, numerous thin sparkling bangles that would reach to both elbows and some soft red beautifully embroidered shoes.

"The shawl can go over you head for the first part of the wedding" Sharmila advised. "I'll help you. Please come to my flat in town tomorrow to get dressed for the wedding. I have never had a daughter to share fashion with and it would be a honour to have you in my home and help you to dress."

Without hesitation I replied. "Sharmila I would love to get ready and dressed to go to my wedding from your home. I'd be thrilled for your help and advice on how the clothes should be worn. Only one request. I want my Mum to be there with us." Sharmila was overjoyed. So that was agreed.
It seemed that Sharmila had gone to a lot of trouble for me and my confidence in our relationship grew stronger. It even felt like I was family. All had been forgiven and me, originally the piggy in the middle, had been accepted.

"We shall, of course, have Haldi" announced Sharmila with great authority. "Tomorrow, on the morning of the wedding, the pair of you will use a mixture of turmeric and rose water and have a kind of play fight."

Rishi had already told me about this turmeric mustard coloured tradition. Turmeric is apparently a well respected sacred spice. It is mentioned in the Hindu scriptures and is a plant related to the ginger family. Turmeric represents prosperity and the start of a new life together. It wards off evil spirits too. "I'll have to have some of that" I joked. "A yellow paste is made up and you will smear it on each other, both of you trying to avoid the paste." advised Sharmila laughing. "Rishi's friends will join in too." She was very proud of her Indian traditions.

"I'll go along with it and give it my best shot" I said confidently. It sounds fun and I want to join in and enjoy everything."

"After Haldi you both shall have Mehndi." Sharmila explained. " It is a form of body art originating from ancient India in which decorative designs are created on your body. You will have beautiful, delicate, ornate henna patterns painted on your hands, arms and feet. I think you will love it Leah. In Rajasthan sometimes men join in this tradition too so hopefully Rishi will be a good sport. I have two top Mehndi artists arriving at 11 o'clock for that purpose." It all sounded absolutely wonderful. With the arrangements finalised we left to return to our hotel and chill out in the spa. Time to relax, as tomorrow would be an amazing day. "Let's both settle down now Leah. You need all your energy for tomorrow." Rishi opted for a hot stone massage and I sunk into the ornate marble warm Jacuzzi. A candle-lit dinner for two and plans for an early night completed a perfect day. It was hard to sleep due to the excitement.

I went over the day in my head, reliving every moment. The heat, the vibrant colours, the relief and fresh air at the hill station, the hustle and bustle of Jaipur, the promised Haldi and Mehndi treats, the beautiful dress, accessories and the excitement. It was such a lot to take in. At about two in the morning I eventually managed to drift off to sleep .

CHAPTER 40

The big day

The next morning came all too quickly. "Rise and shine. Mrs Jain. "Rishi called from the elaborate bathroom. "It's your wedding day" he laughed.

We hurriedly dressed and had breakfast as the taxi was ordered for 8.30am. I had a lot to take, my hot brush, my make up, some new lacy underwear, my oldest trousers and tee shirt for the Haldi fun with the turmeric paste. "I'm putting in a comfy pair of fancy shoes for emergencies Rishi. Nobody will notice if I'm forced to wear these for comfort and I can dance in these if it comes to it." "OK Leah. Good idea. Nothing worse than aching feet and it's going to be a wonderful but tough day"

We arrived, at Rishi's parents flat with Mum in tow. Sharmila greeted us. She was so excited. "Today is a day that I have been dreaming about since my Rishi was born. One door is closing but another is opening."
Pradeep came into the room and we gave each other a warm hug. "Let the Haldi fun begin" he said. "Let's mix the Haldi paste Rishi, but first of all rub this oil on your skin so that the turmeric is easy to wash off. We can't have you going to the wedding looking yellow. " We have some of your closest friends coming to join the fun." Once they had prepared the Haldi paste it was put in a beautiful brass bowl on a tray and rose petals were placed around it.

The friends arrived dressed so that they too could join the fun and get in a mess. Rishi warmly welcomed each of them. It had been a long time since he had been in their company. "Leah. These are the friends that I would play with in the holidays, when I came back from boarding school. They are all my true mates."

Sharmila entered the room with a smile on her face. "You are not doing this indoors boys" she said laughing.

They took the paste carefully to a large square of grass outside the flats and soon it was a free for all. We were laughing so much that people were looking over their balconies doubled up and cheering at the fun we were having. Pradeep videoed the whole scene. I got caught in the middle of the activity and soon we were all covered. It was in our hair, in our mouths and any patch of naked skin was covered.

"Enough." Rishi said in a commanding voice. "Some of us have to get married later today." The friends dispersed as they too had to get ready for the celebration. We went indoors for showers and put on dressing gowns in preparation for the Mehndi body art.
The Mehndi artists both arrived and using a deep coloured henna paste skilfully began making beautiful intricate patterns on our feet and arms with henna. It was an interesting experience that Rishi took part in too. I had always loved the look and tradition. To be part of it myself was an honour. Rishi had told me that a deeper colour meant stronger love and he said that he wanted the henna as deep as possible. Such a romantic.

The finished result was a beautiful work of art with my hands, arms and feet covered in a stunning elaborate designs. "Take some close up photos, Rishi please. I want to show my friends back home.

Sharmila and Pradeep had planned everything well and had left no stone unturned.

A light lunch prepared by Sharmila's housekeeper was enjoyed in a celebratory atmosphere. It was then time to get dressed and return to our hotel for the wedding.

Important basic preparations first! I carefully used my

heated brush to make my hair look its best. I then applied my make up. Just enough to look classy.

The essentials completed I stepped into the dress. It felt quite an emotional experience. Sharmila helped me with the fastenings. "It suits you down to the earth that we walk on Leah" his mother said. Sharmila then showed me how to wear the shawl. She fixed the headdress on me and some huge gold earrings that matched a beautiful turquoise and coral necklace. To complete the jewellery look I added lots of bangles on both arms. "These belonged to my family and are very old" she said. "I'm thrilled to wear them. They are beautiful" I replied. I slipped into some red embroidered soft shoes and took a look at myself in a long mirror. The effect was amazing. I was glowing. Mum hadn't wanted to see me until I was fully dressed and as she came into the room I did a little twirl. Her smile said it all. "Oh Leah. You look wonderful" she said reaching for her tissues as she gave me a cuddle. "Thank you for everything you have done for me, Sharmila." I said. "Yes," agreed Mum. "You have excelled. She looks stunning."

Rishi was in another room dressing and when he opened the door I couldn't believe my eyes. He had a red turban with a long trailing scarf at the back. It really suited him. His silk cream jacket, a flattering and perfect fit, was adorned with shiny gold button and a belt. It was lavish, rich and heavily embroidered. His churidar, silk pyjama trousers, fell into as tightly fitting cuff at the ankle. A fine pair of embroidered soft gold shoes completed the outfit. He looked wonderful. "How is that then Mrs Jain? "Rishi teased. "You look amazing Rishi" I replied. "I'm being blessed with the most handsome Indian in town." "And I am blessed with the most beautiful Indian bride" he said..... "Come on. Let's get married again!"

There was the sound of a horn outside and we looked out. "The cars are here to take you to the Chamu Palace" said Pradeep. "Mum, please share our car."

Two white open-topped Rolls Royce cars gracefully pulled up adorned with a large floral arrangement placed on each bonnet.

'I've not seen that done before,' I thought. Rishi and I went in the first car together. It was my only time in a Rolls Royce, so smooth, elegant and comfortable.

At the hotel we could see a huge crowd. As we drove through the grand hotel gates our drivers began hooting their car horns repeatedly, as if to start the celebtions. The swarm of guests were eagerly awaiting our arrival. The sun had even come out to welcome us. It was such a colourful scene with everyone excited and looking fabulous in their finery. The guest's saris were of every imaginable colour, creating a vibrant scene and the sunshine caught the beading and rich embroidery making them glisten.

A band of drummers and brass players were enthusiastically whipping up the crowd at the entrance to the Chomru Palace Hotel.

As we got out of the cars the crowd cheered excitedly and began to gyrate to the beat of the drums. Arms were waving as people of all ages excitedly danced their socks off. What a wonderful, vivid and noisy greeting. The drummers and guests escorted us towards the hotel. I was speechless. I hadn't expected anything like this. It was a wonderful beginning.

With complete and utter surprise Rishi spotted Monica and Guy in the crowd. "Over there, Leah. Look who has come to our wedding. Isn't that great." The couple had made a special journey from New York. We were shocked but delighted to see them. Guy called over to us. Over the beating of the drums he called out. "How could we have missed all this. It's an experience of a lifetime?"

It turned out that Rishi's parents had got on really well with Monica and Guy. They were all much the same age and had kept in touch. Pradeep had invited them to our wedding as a special surprise for us which had been kept a secret.

A huge tent called a mandap had been erected close to the restaurant entrance. It had widths of bright orange and red pleated cloth forming a roof and was highly decorated with chains of beautiful hanging flowers. There was some impressive red seat-ing and a kind of stage with two enormous thrones for us, the bride and groom. We climbed the steps and excitedly took our seats. Rishi was given a symbolic milk and honey drink.

The priest greeted us and shook our hands. A prayer was offered to Lord Ganesh, to bless the occasion and to remove any obstacles from the ceremony.

Rishi and I exchanged colourful garlands of flowers which hung around our necks. These signified the agreement to our marriage.

We lit a small Holy fire to pray for a happy future.

Now it was time for the priest to perform an important service known as Saat Phere. This is the point in the Hindu religion where seven vows are made by walking round the Holy fire seven times together, so to bind us as a couple.

The vows were offered to bring to the marriage food and nourishment, strength, prosperity, progeny, health and finally the seventh vow which is for a life of love, friendship and trust.

I was really impressed with the significance of the vows which included everything that a happy marriage should be. We felt fulfilled and so happy, now bonded for a lifetime. It had been an honour to be part of this traditional service.

Fortunately any threat of a monsoon held off while the wedding service had taken place. A chance had been taken but luck had prevailed.

The band and the drums struck up again rhythmically as we snaked our way into the reception.

The bar was opened and a lavish banquet was served in the decadent restaurant.

There were an abundance of creamy curries, rice dishes, tandoori meats, buttery naans, paneer and fruits. One after another the dishes were skilfully served by a band of experienced waiters until everyone was satisfied and full to the brim.

It had been a chance for the Chomru Palace to excel, and so it had.

Rishi and I wandered round and chatted to the guests, welcoming them and thanking them for coming. Lovely compliments were exchanged. My Indian wedding attire was given approval by the guests, as was Rishi's wonderful outfit.

We mingled, trying to capture a few words with everyone, if only for a short exchange.

Rishi's mother fussed around us making sure that her upmarket friends had the chance to meet us. "These are our very best friends Rishi. Abhi is banker and Simmi is his wife. They live in Agra." Rishi nodded politely and shook their hands.

His mother loved to impress. Throughout the whole reception people were snapping photos on their 'phones while two official photographers took videos and photographs to provide memories of the occasion. At one point I popped to the toilet. A stunning young lady in a lime green and gold sari came in behind me. She smiled. I was washing my hands when our eyes met in the mirror above the sink.

"Leah, I am Anneka. I am here with my mother, brothers and sisters. As you may know my departed father was a great friend of Pradeep."

With great surprise to myself I turned impulsively to Anneka and gave her a huge hug.

"Anneka, it is so lovely to meet you in person. I'm thrilled that things finally worked out for all of us. You finding true love with somebody else was a great result. The arranged marriage problem was causing a serious rift with Rishi's family but that is all in the past now. It was helped along by the meeting you took the time to have with Rishi's parents, explaining your side of the story. I can't thank you enough."

Anneka spoke gently. "I'm getting married myself, in September. I am to marry the love of my life, a most wonderful man called Barindra. We are deeply in love and meant for each other."

I took her hand. "I'm really happy for you. I hope that you have a wonderful wedding and a long and happy marriage. Good Luck to you both." We gave each other a meaningful hug. Things could have turned out so differently.

Following the meal the crowd moved into the opulent banqueting hall for the dancing and party. Rishi and I, hand in hand, watched the evenings events unfolding.

A stage had been erected at one end. Arches of beautiful fresh flowers decorated the stage. The loud and somewhat sharp brass band struck up the music and on the stage came a group of young men, including Archan. They looked wonderful, all dressed alike, with their pink turbans and silver grey silk suits. I quickly realised they were Rishi's childhood friends, the ones that Rishi called his true mates.

They had prepared a choreographed dance to entertain the guests as a surprise. In unison they delivered some impressive entertainment which included amazing somersaults and back-bends. The guests went absolutely wild, whooping with delight and shouting "more, more." It had gone down a treat.

This stunning performance was followed by a female singer with a beautiful voice, accompanied by three backing singers. They were all dressed to impress, glittering in their sparkling silk saris as they performed to their audience.

After the soft, serious traditional song the mood changed quickly and unexpectedly. The music amplified as the singers became dancers, gyrating in unison in true Bollywood style. They took the onlookers by storm. It was magnificent. A real show stopper.

for the guests to get up and dance, and dance they did. "Come on, Mrs Jain, onto the dance floor" said Rishi. So we danced our socks off together till we could dance no more. The whole room was shaking with the sound of the traditional music ringing out and everyone loved it.

Regardless of age they danced. Men with their hands on their hips swaying enthusiastically to the music. Many going round and round in circles waving their arms high in the air. Mum got into the swing of things copying the best dancers. "I didn't know Mum could move like that " I said laughing.

Sharmila came up to us. "Well, what do you think of your wedding? I hope that you are enjoying the celebrations. Your father and I felt that it was right to give you all the traditions for your Indian wedding, especially as you had come from England."Rishi replied. "Mother. This is perfect for us. We love it all. Thank you so much for everything. We wouldn't be in the fortunate position that we are in today if it hadn't been for you and my father." Sharmila smiled. " You both deserve it. You make a lovely couple." With that she happily danced away, arms in the air waving, hips swaying to the beat of the music." Time for the cake " she called.

Rishi and I then cut a six tiered wedding cake which had been brought onto the stage. The guests cheered and more 'photos were taken as we gave each other a taste before it was served to the guests.

More dancing followed. A host of colourful balloons dropped from the ceiling and bags of confetti were given out to the guests. The children, as you might imagine, enjoyed throwing the confetti around and the excitement was apparent.

The grand finale of the wedding was a spectacular firework display on the hotel lawns. "I love you so much" said Rishi. We held each other tight, watching rockets soaring into the night sky, one after another.

Back in the banqueting hall guests assembled and formed an arch for Rishi and I to pass through before leaving the celebrations. The brass band struck up again for a final time playing an old English song, 'Goodnight Ladies.' A lovely touch.

We could not have asked for better. Rishi's parents had been more than generous and given us a fantastic wedding. All this and they had managed to keep much of it a surprise.

CHAPTER 41

The following day

The next two days were spent at our plush hotel enjoying its facilities, a perfect opportunity to recover from the celebrations.

On our first morning we mulled over the wedding with a jug of fresh coffee served on the lawn. Rishi explained his relationship with the guests, both friends and family, so that I understood more about the guests that I had been introduced to. We talked about what fun it had all been, pleased that everything had gone so well.

The hotel provided us with a well needed rest as both Rishi and I were exhausted from work, the new home and lifestyle, plus the travelling.

Rishi had a relaxing massage at the spa and we both went for refreshing swims and soaks in the Jacuzzi. We relaxed on the lawns with champagne and generally chilled out.

Later that day we were able to view the video and photos and relive the experience.

I told Rishi of my chance meeting with Anneka and how happy she had seemed. "I am pleased that the two of you met" said Rishi. "That saga is all in the past now, thank goodness."

Mum had two days of sightseeing thoughtfully planned by-Rishi's parents on a private tour. She would be seeing some striking architecture within the extensive palace complexes and have the opportunity to delve deeply into Jaipur's culture and history. Mum loved anything like that.

Later that day Monica and Guy joined us. They had enjoyed a jeep ride to Fort Amber, a classic, romantic Rajasthani Fort Palace. "Wonderful " drawled Monica.

Soon after, Mum returned and told us excitedly about their trip. "Amazing" said Mum. "So grateful to Sharmila and Pradeep for arranging this for me and we really enjoyed each others company."

Rishi ordered more champagne and we played a few traditional games. One Indian wedding game determined who would take charge in the relationship. Rishi and I had to take off our rings and put them in a pot of clear water. As the rings settled to the bottom, we were asked to churn the water as vigorously as possible. Once his or her hands came out, everyone looked at the water. If the bride's ring lags behind in the swirling water she will be an obedient wife. If it is the opposite, the groom will be wrapped around her finger. It was just a bit of fun as we would be having an equal relationship. I didn't believe in being subservient in our marriage.
Rishi wouldn't have wanted that and he lost the game anyway.

Guy and Pradeep had discovered the hotel's snooker table so sneaked off for a game before Sharmila noticed.

One of Rishi's best friends turned up and the pair of them went to play tennis on the hotel's courts while those who remained chatted as dusk fell.

Our last day, before travelling home was spent in the same vein, reviving and enjoying the hotel facilities.

That evening we went to a top vegetarian restaurant that Pradeep used regularly. It had won the town's Certificate of Excellence, a well deserved award. Monica and Guy had been invited too.

Archan arrived unexpectedly. " I'm not going to miss out when there is good food about" he said.

Archan was an interesting young man. He worked for his father, helping to run the successful spice business. Like Rishi he had been well educated at the upmarket school in Somerset but had returned after A levels. Archan had gone on to University in India before settling in Mumbai. He spent his spare time volunteering at a youth club where he ran the football and cricket teams. Archan was sports mad. "We have been training very hard. I have about forty regular boys at the club. They are mainly from poor families and the club gives them a focus and a place to meet. Focussing on sport helps to keep them out of trouble. There are a couple of brilliant runners who we are hoping will get a place to represent India in the next Olympic Games. They are training for the marathon." "Wow, that's an achievement. Well done Archan" I said. "I am sure that you appreciate how lucky you have been with your education and job in your fathers business. It is nice to be able to give something back."

The next words Archan spoke took Rishi and I completely by surprise.
"Not sure if you both know this but Lynne, your bridesmaid and I have kept in touch and I have been invited to stay with

her family for Christmas. Although I was educated in England, I never actually spent Christmas there. It will be a great experience to see a real decorated Christmas tree, pull crackers and eat Mince Pies. I was always back in India for the long holidays. When Christmas is over we are planning to go to the Lake District where my parents stayed before your Blackpool wedding. They said the scenery is stunning. We both love the English countryside and we will spend New Year hill walking. We have made a list of the places we want to see. Lynne particularly wants to visit Hilltop, Beatrix Potter's home. I would love to climb Helvellyn, weather permitting and visit some of the lakes like Buttermere and Windermere. I'm not looking forward to is the cold weather." He laughed.

He was such a personable young man. "You need to buy some thermal undies." I said jokingly." They will keep you warm. The Lake District is beautiful at any time of year. Have fun."

Guy got to his feet to make a speech. He loved to be the life and soul. "I'd like to toast the new Mr. and Mrs. Jain and wish them all the best in their new life together. May all their troubles be little ones."

We laughed. 'Little ones' subtly referred to Rishi and I having a family of our own! Not quite ready for that yet.

Guy continued. "I'd also like to thank Rishi's parents for inviting Monica and I to experience the traditions of an Indian wedding. It has been superb, an experience of a lifetime. I hope that we can continue with our friendship and return the favour. I want here and now to invite them both to stay at our home in New York. They are welcome anytime...... and I mean it."

A round of applause went up and Rishi's parents looked more than pleased. Rishi then though that perhaps he ought to give a vote of thanks too. He could speak off the cuff and make a good job of it. He rose from his chair. "My wife and I," they laughed, "want to thank my parents Sharmila and Pradeep for arranging such a wonderful and generous wedding for us. You may know that we left the arrangements in their hands and merely asked them to surprise us. So surprise us they did. We could not have asked for better. Our Hindu wedding has been an amalgamation of tradition, religion, language, architecture, culture, food, customs, dance and music. I could go on..... Leah and I have loved every minute. We will take our memories back to our new home in Preston and the start of our new life together. Thank you all for making it such fun for us and for being part of it. We love you all Thank You to Leah's mother for giving me her beautiful daughter to be my wife."

A loud, happy cheer filled the room. Guy, obviously , once again a little the worse for drink, asked everyone to hold up their napkin and wave it around while he sang. Naturally we all obliged. He was word perfect and gave quite a good rendition of the old Cliff Richard's hit song, 'Congratulations'. It was a wonderful end to a lovely evening.

CHAPTER 42

The shock

We arrived back home to Preston safely and soon got into the swing of working in our new jobs, meeting new people, having new neighbours and generally getting into a routine.

Mum and I met up about once a week, usually on my day off. Mum had a full time job but used any flexi time owing to get together. We would have coffee at Lytham St Annes, walk along the front, perhaps have fish and chips and get our shopping for the week on the way back.

Mum would come back to mine for dinner, see Rishi and drive herself home. It was an uneventful yet comfortable routine.

It occurred to me that since my marriage I had not been back to Mum's except to chat at the door or pick her up. It was only after my big shock that I realised this was the case.

It was getting cold now and there was a distinct chill in the air in the mornings. Winter was well and truly with us with Christmas just around the corner.

One morning the 'phone rang. It was Mum. She sounded worried.

"Morning Leah. Instead of our usual can we go somewhere different today? I have something to tell you. I'll be with you in half an hour. Not sure what you will say but brace yourself. Must go and get ready. Bye."

What was that about, I wondered? I hated this 'not knowing' kind of message and I didn't even get a chance to speak. I hope that Mum's not ill or something really serious has happened. Why all this mystery? Couldn't she have just told me over the 'phone?

I sat down for a few minutes and ran over a few things in my mind. I had noticed Mum making some discreet calls when we were in India, then there was the time that I overheard her when she had received a call and greeted the person as Darling. It was a mystery to me but my suspicions had been aroused. There were times when I felt she had been holding back with something and times when I could see that she had something on her mind. There was a jigsaw of clues. What about the chest of drawers at Mum's house with men's clothes mysteriously inside? What's my Mum up to?

Mum arrived. Out of the blue she had decided we would go to the Clitheroe Museum, within one hours drive. "Somewhere different" Mum had said. We drove in silence. I tried to ask what this was all about but Mum just said "Not now, later Leah, when the moment is right."

The Museum is set on a hill next to the remains of Clitheroe Castle in the beautiful Ribble Valley. We wandered around the galleries observing eight hundred years of history but Mum had her mind elsewhere.

I was anxious to find out what this was all about but held back. The mood was subdued. Normally Mum would be animated in these surroundings. Not today. There was something serious on her mind.

We headed off to a country pub for lunch and sat at a table by the log fire. Drinks, hot soup and lasagne were ordered. We ate the delicious warming meal, but unusually we didn't chat. Mum was deep in thought.

It was at the end of the meal when Mum came to the point finally plucking up the courage.

"Leah, I need to tell you something. I'm not sure how you will take this as it will come as a shock for you."

I looked at Mum mystified.

"I have been seeing Phil, your old house manager."

This was not what I expected to hear. A new man in her life maybe, but not Phil. It was a lot to take in.

Mum spoke. "You will remember that we got on really well when we went sightseeing in London.

You will recall that he came up to Preston to look at the University. He was so nice to me when we spent a day together.

Well, now it has gone past that. Phil came to lodge with me when he began his Masters course at the University.

I kept it from you as I didn't know how to tell you.

To be perfectly frank Leah, we were attracted to each other. Phil has been living with me, at my house on and off, since well before your wedding. We have spent a lot of time together and we have found that we mean a lot to each other. I know that there is an age difference between us but Phil is mature for his years and I am young for my years. We have sort of met in the middle.

We are now most definitely a couple if you know what I mean.

This is an unusual situation but I hope that you understand."

I sat speechless with shock. It's not the kind of thing you expect to hear from your Mum. The penny dropped.

The men's clothing in the drawer when I stayed with Mum before my Blackpool wedding. The 'phone calls that I overheard. This was who Mumwas speaking to when she when calling someone 'Darling' the 'phone. I had noticed that when we went shopping Mum always seemed to buy a lot of food, but I didn't expect it to be for her lover! Things now began to make sense.

It was a bit like history repeating itself. I needed Rishi's parents approval in my relationship with Rishi and now Mum needed mine. It wouldn't have felt so difficult but way back, before Rishi, I had a soft spot for Phil myself. We shared the house in London, even had a day out together. It hadn't gone any further. "Just as well under the circumstances" I thought.

"I need a bit of time to come to terms with this and I feel quite shocked. Let's go home. I need to mull this over," I said shakily.

Luckily Mum was driving as I don't think I could have driven home safely. We reached my house but Mum didn't want to come in. "No Leah, you go indoors and get your head round this. I know it's a lot to take in but I think that you want me to be happy" she said gently. "Of course, Mum" I whispered back.

That evening, over dinner and an extra large glass of wine, I told Rishi about Mum and her relationship with Phil.

He was as surprised as I was. "She kept that quiet and under wraps." he said." It's not the kind of thing I would have expected from your Mum but, hey, why not? Everyone deserves happiness and it sounds like she has found it. It shows me that we are so happy in our own little bubble that we are not seeing what's happening around us! Good Luck to them" he said meaningfully.

Rishi then went silent for a moment as he thought deeply. Having come to his own conclusions he said "Well really Leah, it's none of our business except that it is your mother. She isn't getting any younger so it will be nice for her to have a partner to go on holidays with. I know that is something she has missed since your father died. She told me so. The age difference doesn't really come into it if they love each other and get on well together. They could have years of enjoying a happy life together, years of holidays in the sun and contentment in a loving home. They can look after and care for each other, growing older together. Let us give them our blessing, like my parents and your Mum gave to us. Let us celebrate their love and be grateful that they found each other."

So that is exactly what we did.

I rang Mum and asked if they'd like to both come round for the evening when I was next off work. It was a bit odd hen I saw Phil at first. He looked a lot older and had put on a bit of weight but to compensate he seemed happier and more open and light hearted, even a different person.

Mum and Phil shared the same sense of humour, enjoyed the same kind of things, history, country walks, nature, holidays and music.

Phil explained that the course at the University was working out well. He had made a lot of good contacts, was doing well on the

Masters course and had been approached about a management job in the music industry, just like he wanted. It would start at the end of the course.

The work would probably take him back to London. I reeled at this. Mum going to leave Blackpool to live in London?

The tables had turned full circle. I would miss her dreadfully but I thought back to the encouragement she had given me when I left Blackpool for a new start and really there was no difference. Mum would be doing what she wanted. It would be a fresh start for her and she would love all that London offers. The culture, theatres, museums, the night life, the ethnic restaurants, the countryside on the doorstep and the wonderful characters from every country in the world in one big melting pot.

We raised our glasses "To the happy couple. Long may it last." We all hugged. So that brings me to the end of my story...... and the beginning of an exciting new one for Mum and Phil.

Just one last bit of really important news. After Christmas Lynne contacted me to say that she and Archan had got engaged after their break in the Lake District.

They had treasured every moment of their perfect time in this stunning and romantic part of the world. Archan had proposed to Lynne on New Years Eve, round a cosy fire, in a country pub, on the stroke of midnight and on one knee!
"It was so exciting. I didn't know anything about it" she gushed. "I'm so in love. We just can't wait to get married."

I replied, tongue in cheek with something that Lynne always said to me. "It is in the stars. Your life is already planned."

Printed in Great Britain
by Amazon